Connection

ELISE

Katharine E. Smith

HEDDON PUBLISHING

www.heddonpublishing.com
www.facebook.com/heddonpublishing
@PublishHeddon

Katharine E. Smith is the author of eleven novels, including the bestselling Coming Back to Cornwall series.

Elise is the first book of the Connections series – also set in Cornwall but quite different.

A Philosophy graduate, Katharine initially worked in the IT and charity sectors. She turned to freelance editing in 2009, which led to her setting up Heddon Publishing, working with independent authors across the globe.

Katharine lives in Shropshire, UK, with her husband, their two children, and their border collie.

You can find details of her books on her website:
www.katharineesmith.com

Information about her work with other authors can be found here:
www.heddonpublishing.com
and
www.heddonbooks.com

For the dads: Ted, Barry – and of course Chris.

And for my super-cool, super-strong friend, Laura.

Love, always.

ELISE

Open the window.

Up the stairs,
Through bedrooms,
Into the attic.
Pulling back curtains, carpets, floorboards.
Peeling back covers,
Blowing off dust,
Polishing glass till it gleams.

Elise

It's a good day today. I can see from the way the girl chats
to her mum, hanging on to her hand as they make their
way along the street, unaware as always that they are
being observed. The girl has barely drawn breath and her
mother is looking at her fondly, cheeks dimpled as she
smiles down at her daughter, nodding at something the
girl's saying.

They must be quite new in town. I first noticed them
walking by my place last September, and I'm fairly sure
they live in one of the terraces tucked away behind the
chippy. I've watched their progress. To and fro. Monday
to Friday, day in, day out, through all types of weather,
appearances changing accordingly, from short-sleeved
summer dresses, faces red and shiny in the heat, to
bundles of coats, scarves and gloves, heads down against
the stiff wind blowing straight off the sea.

The town is in want of some TLC. Has been for some
time. Not like our upmarket neighbour; a sparkling
holiday resort, its fortunes once tied with ours, but the
influx of artists combined with the aesthetically pleasing
twisty cobbled streets and three clean, sheltered beaches
with friendly waters, saw it nose ahead at first, then take

flying leaps into the world of tourism. Flooding with upmarket self-catering properties and posh-looking restaurants, while our town was left somewhat lacking. I prefer it that way, though, and many of us feel the same. But that is all set to change.

Someone, somewhere – I fight the urge to think *London* with the obligatory disapproving tone – for one thing, I'm from London, though that was many moons ago – has decided to invest in the town. In the harbour. A shabby, but charming for its very shabbiness, working harbour. Free of yachts and pleasure vessels for the most part. Now being offered up to a *development*. The Saltings. We had a talk about it at the club. A lovely young woman from the company doing the developing had come along with a little model for us all to look at, and lots of nice smiles while she explained how fantastic this was going to be for the town. ("Sweet-talk us old thickos," Bill had whispered to me, and I'd nudged him to keep quiet. After all, the girl was only doing her job.)

A selection of exclusive waterfront properties. A cinema, bowling lanes, and an indoor surf training school. What on earth would we need that for, when the sea is right outside? A chain coffee shop and a couple of those restaurants you get at every out-of-town leisure place. Chiquitos, is it? And that Italian one.

As a nod to the town, there were talks underway with the fishing community to see that they were provided for, and construction of supposedly affordable housing (not the waterfront ones, of course, which are not going to be affordable by many people's standards).

It makes me shudder. Thinking again of the neighbouring town; though its skeleton remains in place, it's grown, puffed out with new housing developments further uphill, and blocks of fancy apartments or flash modern houses springing up wherever a street once paused for breath. There is barely a day that goes by when the sound of building work can't be heard.

It's not that I can't face change. Not at all. I completely understand that change is a necessity. No, it's the money that gets me. The ease with which people breeze in, make their plans, make their homes – or second, even third and fourth – claiming the landscape without a care in the world, money flowing through their fingers like seawater. Effortlessly taking the best of the views, and blocking the cherished, sacred light of that place; not to mention the possibility of locals not being able to afford to live in their own town.

It's no use being stuck in the past; I know that only too well. And I'm not a local, not by birth – I'm from London, remember? – although I've lived here for nearly eighty years, so I do feel some kind of right to an opinion, at the very least. But what I don't feel is that righteous indignation of some of the folks at the club, most of whom I've known for decades.

Sometimes I find it hard to believe that I can possibly have known anybody for tens of years. But a glance in the mirror – or a kindly-meant look, or shouted word (why do younger people assume all older people must be hard of hearing?), in a shop or on the street – is a sharp reminder of my age.

My own house is small, and basic. Three small bedrooms and a tiny bathroom upstairs. A kitchen and a lounge and a little utility room pinned onto the back downstairs. A smallish garden, with vegetable plots in raised beds, built by my son to save my back. It may not be luxurious, or particularly modern, but it is home. There's no price that can be put on that.

My home, where I have lived since my children were small, where we moved to not long after I became a single mother (*widowed mother*, I remind myself – as if that makes any difference to anything), is a house with a bit of a view. On a narrow terrace, which curves away uphill, from my front windows I can see the sea. Downstairs, I can see a sliver of the long, sweeping beach in one direction, and the harbour, the heart of the town, in the other. The sound of the sea, which sinks into the background like water into sand. Unobtrusive, yet always there.

In the summer, the breeze carries the noise of the holidaymakers, who pack the soft sands, colouring in the view from my bedroom window, which has a better outlook on it all. Windbreaks, tents, bright beach towels, kites, umbrellas, in every shade under the sun.

I steer clear myself these days; I would be out of place in that scene, I'm sure. But I enjoy hearing it. Can well imagine it all. Spray-soaked, salty-skinned children, wet hair stuck to their faces, not caring about the sand that invades their lunches, a soft but sure crunch with each bite. Pale-skinned adults, having shrugged off their day-to-day business suits and sensible shoes, relishing the feel of sand between their toes and sun on their skin. Trousers rolled up, if they don't feel too daring, or just not caring, baring their skin to the world.

Lunchtime beers in the midday sun. Bottles of pop, sweating with condensation. Ice cream drips, licked from sticky lips. Wetsuits and body boards, buckets and spades. One week for these people, or two if they are very lucky, to cram in as much carefreeness as possible.

I'm glad that they can; I like to hear their shrieks and shouts, imagine their abandon. I know that when autumn approaches and the tide of holidaymakers starts to slide away, the town is still ours.

Every day, I can see the sea, without leaving my house. I can hear it when I'm sleeping. I can feel it in the air that creeps in through my permanently open bedroom window. And I know all its faces, all its moods, and I know I am lucky. No matter how angry it gets. *You don't scare me,* I scold it – but only in my head. I haven't lost my marbles enough to actually speak the words out loud. Not yet.

There was a time I would be in and out of the waves every day, given half a chance. When I close my eyes, I can re-live that feeling still; the absolute joy of the saltwater splashing my face, skin prickling with goose bumps at the shock of the cold. When the children were small; after their dad was gone, of course. An idyllic day spent at the beach, usually with friends – more often than not, Maudie and Fred. Running up the steps that have been carved into the rocks at the very end of the beach. Across the road, into the house and hastily building sandwiches on the wooden chopping board, slipping them into a paper bag, refilling flasks, then back down to the sand again. Now, of course, my children are long grown up and far away.

The things I've seen, I think, as I watch the mother and daughter continue their journey, hand-in-hand.

I am unseen, unnoticed, and I like it in many ways, but I know that in recent years I have pulled back from the world. What would the little girl think, if she noticed me? What would she see? An old lady, of little interest or relevance to her immediate, urgent, vibrant world. Maybe that's how it should be.

The mum might be different; she'd see an old lady, too, but I would put money on this woman being a little more in tune with things; and a little more aware that one day she too will be an old lady – that all the things she's been through in her younger years will seem irrelevant to most people. But she will also have the luxury, as I do now, of picking and choosing. Breathing life into cherished memories, and doing her best to keep away from the times she would rather forget.

1939

One of the times Elise Morgan would never forget, and had no wish to, was her first glimpse of the town. From her seat in a train carriage especially commissioned for the school, she was one of the few quiet ones, who had stopped chatting long enough to notice the sheer turquoise of the sea, and the houses that tumbled down the streets towards the harbour, orange-lichened roofs and white walls soaking up the light of the sun. Glowing.

It was incredible, really, Elise had thought, how happy and excited her schoolmates were. And these were the ones who had wailed on the platform as they said goodbye to parents or, in some cases, nannies. Really, for most of them, it was little different to being sent away to the normal school. It may have been much further away from family homes, but it was unlikely they would have seen anything more of their parents had they been any closer. Even at the age of ten, Elise was aware that many of her counterparts enjoyed melodrama, and attention-seeking. She shied away from it, and from many of them. But her eyes had met those of Violet Wetherbourne, who had also been sitting quietly – reading, mostly – while the train slowly rattled its way from the South East to the South West, showcasing the coast and the lines of golden-sanded beaches, now bearing ugly scars of barbed-wire defences. Violet, one of the other very young girls, would feel much as Elise did. The tight, twisted stomach as the train carried them into the unknown.

The pace slowed, and the sound of the heavy brakes reverberated through the carriages. Imogen, who was twelve, and in Elise's opinion one of the main attention-seekers, exclaimed, "Oh, but isn't it absolutely *glorious!*" Adding, with a sob for good measure, "But I miss Mummy so much."

Violet's eyes met Elise's again, then rolled in their sockets, momentarily coming back to rest at cross-eyed. Elise grinned, and stuck her tongue out towards Imogen's back; currently being rubbed by one of her hangers-on, who was anxiously trying to reassure her. Elise would put money – if she had any – on Imogen being absolutely fine again in moments. Or on second thoughts, maybe not until the bedrooms had been allotted and she had secured the room, and the bed, and the room-mates, of her choice.

"Come on, girls, time waits for no man! Or girl," Miss Forbes called, casting a smile Elise's way.

Miss Forbes was the English teacher, who caused many a raised eyebrow amongst staff and parents for her insistence on wearing men's pedal-pushers each and every day. She was 'thoroughly modern', as Elise's mother, Annabel, approvingly said, and each year she involved all the girls in an end-of-year play.

'Failed actress' was one of the less flattering descriptions Elise had heard muttered amongst her schoolmates; no doubt a second-hand opinion learned from uncharitable parents.

At the thought of her mother, Elise's stomach clenched even more tightly. She had never known her father and, with no brothers or sisters, it had only ever been just her and her mum. Annabel was herself a thoroughly modern woman, although her calling had been to the medical profession – a very different kind of theatre to that of

Miss Forbes. She hadn't wanted her daughter to leave her, but when Elise achieved the full scholarship to the Whiteley School for Girls, she couldn't help but be delighted.

"You did it!" she'd cried, clasping Elise by her cheeks so hard that it nearly hurt. "I'm so proud! This is the beginning of a better future for you, my love."

Her enthusiasm had been infectious, and it wasn't until late that night, tucked up in the bed that the two of them shared in their tiny flat, that Elise began to wonder if going away to school was for her, after all. All her friends were at the local school, and she wondered what the other girls would be like, at this new place. She had been there on the train with Annabel, for an interview, and to do some tests, and it had taken her breath away. It was like no school she had ever seen before, with its tall, stately towers and cool wooden interiors adorned by old, dark paintings of the building's previous occupants.

The Whiteley School for Girls was housed in a stately home not far from London. Whiteley Hall had been transformed into a school by the lady of the house. The lord of the manor had died young and Lady Whiteley, along with her trusted housekeeper, Mrs Emily Hazlehurst, had become deeply involved in the politics of the Suffragettes. This fostered high aspirations, for the world to change for women, and when Emily's daughter Mary was old enough, Lady Whiteley sponsored her to train as a teacher, whilst behind the scenes plans were made for a small school to be set up in what had been the chapel. Mary came back to work at Whiteley, teaching a small group of local girls. From this first intake came two more teachers. Lady Whiteley died, entrusting the Hall to Emily and Mary, and a board of trustees, who quickly enacted her wishes in transforming the house into a permanent school. Girls now came from far and wide, or at least from across the Home Counties, the majority of families paying for their daughters' education, but there were local day girls, who were offered an unconditional place, irrespective of family income, as had been Lady Whiteley's wish. There were also girls from further afield, who could be offered a scholarship. It had been Miss Forbes, who was a friend of Annabel's, who had suggested Elise apply.

Emily had died in the late 1920s, but Mary stayed on at Whiteley, taking on the role of headmistress. She relished the chance to see the girls learning, and dedicated herself fully to the school's running and development.

It was Mary, or Miss Hazlehurst, as the girls knew her, who had seen through the idea of a scholarship for girls from urban areas. She had lived and trained in London, and seen what life was like there, in comparison to that of the wealthy country girls who were the norm when it came to boarders, and even how different it was to that of the local day girls, who at least had the benefit of fresh air and open spaces. A scholarship would not be offered to just anyone, however. As well as the exam, an interview was required, and thus it was that at the tender age of nine, Elise had found herself racked with nerves at the gate to Whiteley School for Girls.

Miss Forbes had been waiting to welcome Elise and Annabel, and quickly put them both at ease.

"Come in, take a seat," she had smiled kindly at Elise.

"We will ask you in for the interview first, then to take the paper, and then, when you're out of the woods, one of our older girls will show you around."

Annabel had asked questions, about previous pupils, and what they had done after leaving the school. On hearing that more than a few had gone on to university, she had smiled, apparently satisfied that this might be the place for her daughter's academic development. Meanwhile, Elise had sat upright on her chair, her hands tucked under her thighs. She could feel the hard outline of the leather seat, digging into her skin. Her palms were sweaty, from nerves and from the weight of her legs.

A grandfather clock counted time in the corner, each tick so loud it played on Elise's nerves, and she could have jumped each time she heard it. But she breathed long and deeply, as Annabel had taught her, and soon enough it was time for her interview.

There were two ladies on the other side of the desk: Miss Forbes, who was the deputy headmistress, and Miss Hazlehurst, the headmistress, who was quite prim and proper but who smiled benevolently at Elise and listened eagerly to her answers. In fact, her gaze was so intense, even when she was smiling, that it made Elise more self-conscious. She felt that something was expected of her, but she wasn't sure quite what it was.

Nevertheless, Miss Forbes asked questions in such a way that she found in time she relaxed, and was able to answer openly, but politely.

"What are your favourite subjects, Elise?"

"I enjoy everything at school, but I love English."

Miss Forbes had smiled and Elise knew it was the right answer for her. "Anything else?" she had prompted.

"I do like mathematics, and we have done some science, which I think is very interesting. We learned about measuring liquids, and we tested the rainfall in the school playground, and..." Elise had surprised herself in the free rein of her answer and, suddenly self-conscious again, the words drained away.

"That sounds very interesting," Miss Forbes had smiled.

"And tell me, Elise," Miss Hazlehurst said, "do you enjoy physical activity? Swimming, for example?"

"Oh, I can't swim, miss. I don't know where we would, round our way. I... I'd like to, I think."

"We are extremely fortunate at Whiteley, to have use of the local public swimming baths on a Wednesday afternoon. You wouldn't be the first girl who has come to us unable to swim. But every girl leaves here a competent swimmer. We pride ourselves, Mrs Morgan, on providing many opportunities for physical education, as well as mental stimulation. Whiteley girls go into the world prepared for anything."

While Annabel smiled and nodded, almost as nervous as her daughter, Elise's mind was full of the idea of swimming... she could hardly imagine it. She knew there was an open-air lido in Hampstead that had recently opened, but she didn't know anybody who used it. She might be the first Whiteley girl to leave unable to swim; unprepared for everything. If she got a place, of course.

"What about running?" Miss Forbes had asked.

Running was something Elise did in the course of games – but did she enjoy it? She supposed so. She thought of running about the local neighbourhood at home, with some of her friends, when they were playing

Hide and Seek or, on the one misjudged occasion she had come to regret, Knock Out Ginger. The breathless exertion and need to stop and catch your breath. Her best friend Susan's eyes shining like the sunshine.

"Yes, I like running," she had answered, and it seemed to please her interviewers. It was only later that she realised people actually ran purely for the sake of running. Short-distance races, and long-distance cross country were regular parts of the Whiteley routine. It had all seemed very strange to her at first.

After the interview, the paper had seemed a doddle and it was just a relief to be able to sit in silence and catch her breath.

Suffice to say, she passed, and the following September she arrived at the school with her new uniform, regulation nightwear and underwear, games kit and so on – all paid for via a voucher scheme. And it had taken quite some time to get used to it all, and to know where she was expected to sit at mealtime, where her classroom was, and her place in the pecking order of the school – not to mention the loneliness of a bed to herself, in a room with three other girls, far away from her mum.

And by and by, she had grown used to it, but then, in her second year there, she and the other girls had been shunted off to Cornwall. Somewhere she had heard of before but knew nothing about. Further away from her mum than ever, and she would have to get used to all the newness, all over again.

Elise

It's not that I can't leave the house. I am perfectly mobile. But somehow, it's harder to find the mental energy these days. It's more difficult to find that impetus when you're alone. And it's not that I wish Davey was still around; he has been dead a long, long time, and I can't say that I ever missed him. It was much worse having to get used to the children growing up and leaving town, although I had felt those apron strings stretch and break a long time before that; particularly with Louisa, whose main driving force seemed to be ensuring she was as little like her mother as possible.

Always a headstrong girl, from about the age of fifteen, Louisa had gone out of her way to make sure she did things differently. She had tried out being a punk, with spiked-up hair and a nose-ring, then a hippy, retaining the nose-ring but losing the dramatic make-up and dying her hair henna-red, letting it grow as long as it wanted. All the while as if I knew nothing of these things; of what it was to be young, the world just a playground.

My daughter had determinedly found older boyfriends to match these images, and seemed disappointed when I had failed to react against these acts of rebellion. Going off to Bristol University at the age of twenty, by the time Louisa returned to Cornwall at Christmas, she was transformed into something like head girl material —

incredibly studious, but sociable and sporty. Not so different to the girl I had been.

Now a very successful and wealthy businesswoman in the City of London, it seems to be a constant source of pain to Louisa that I can never actually get my head around what it is that she does. She studied computer science at university and has worked her way through a range of jobs; each better-paid and with a grander title than the one before, until she has landed a role at the top of an American finance firm, whose headquarters are in some state-of-the-art, sharp-edged offices in central London. I am bowled over by my daughter's intelligence and ambition, but somehow never quite find the right way to get this across to her. Instead, I tell people that Louisa works 'in computers' and if my daughter is within earshot she will roll her eyes – fondly, or in irritation, depending on the day – a clear indication of the depths to which my image has shrunk in my daughter's eyes.

And yet, once we were like that woman and girl who pass by my window. As a child, Louisa was attached to me like a shadow. She had kicked up a fuss being left at school every day, for nearly two years; not because she didn't like school, but because she could not bear to be parted from me. The only other adult she would tolerate was Maudie, my best friend. She more than tolerated her, actually, she loved her like an auntie, and Laurie did, too. Maudie was like family to all of us. Of course, to anyone with half a brain, there must have been some effect on my girl from her dad dying when she was so young, but she couldn't put it into words, and I preferred to go on as if the whole thing had no impact on her. That we were better off without him. I still believe that is true.

Louisa and I would spend hours together on the beach, or in the sea, or tucked up on the window seat, reading books – at first me reading to her, and then, as she grew older, our similar small, neat frames tucked up under either end of a blanket, books transporting us into separate worlds yet firmly sharing the same space. Now, although I know that the love is still there, we just can't seem to find common ground. It could be painful, if I let it, but I prefer to see my daughter for the strident woman she is – forging her way in the male-dominated business world. My mum would have been so proud.

Laurie, though close to his sister, is very different, and entirely driven by love – not of a woman, or a man, but of birds, and now, as a warden on one of the remote Scottish islands, he could not be further away from me while still being on the British Isles. Yet he phones me, if not every day, then every other day. He will tell me about his work, and any rare avian sightings, or marine life, like whales passing by. He's due to retire next year, and not before time. I'm impressed with his resilience, as it's a physical job and he's no longer a young man. He's had more than one opportunity to come back to the mainland, to a comfy office. But that was never his style.

Laurie lives with another warden – a woman called Liz – although, disappointingly, the only passion the two of them seem to share is for wildlife. I sometimes allow my mind to wander and imagine that, on particularly stormy winter nights, when the rest of the world must seem so remote as wind whips the angry sea into a rage and howls around the stone cottage walls, Laurie and Liz might find solace in each other.

It is alien to me that my son doesn't seem to have any

interest in romantic love. He never really seemed to have a love life at all, or at least not one that I knew of. As a teenager, six years older than Louisa, he had been tall and awkward, never knowing that he had those same good looks as his father, which had made Davey the most popular boy in town. It was almost as though Laurie chose to play them down, wearing dowdy clothes; eminently practical for hiking and birdwatching, but highly impractical for attracting any romantic attention. He couldn't be bothered with his hair, which was thick and gingery – the one gift I had imparted in terms of his looks – and which he had cut when he could be bothered, in the cheapest place in town, really just to keep it out of his eyes.

I sometimes found myself wishing my teenage son would put in a bit of effort with his appearance, but at the same time I was annoyed with myself for feeling that way, knowing it was not important what Laurie looked like, but what kind of person he was. After all, his father may have looked the part, but his nature had been far from my quiet, gentle and considered son's. As with Louisa, it is perhaps obvious that some of Laurie's ways are the product of losing his dad so young – and Laurie would have been old enough to remember a little of what his dad was like – but we are all a product of our experiences, both good and bad. It's just that some of us have better experiences than others.

It took me a long time to come to terms with the idea that I would never be a grandmother. And, just when I'd made peace with the idea, along came Ada. Louisa's first and only foray into motherhood, at the age of forty-five.

Named after Ada Lovelace, my granddaughter is intelligent, like her mother – and dark, like Louisa. Like Davey. Possibly like her own father, too. I wouldn't know; I've never met Ada's father, and neither has Ada.

"I knew I wanted a baby," Louisa told me, matter-of-factly. "I never thought I would but then, I did. And so I made it happen." The father didn't come into it, apparently. I am not sure he even knows that he is a father. But his absence from Ada's life has not seemed to have much effect on her. She has grown up tall and strong and confident. She is also an aspiring artist. "Like you, Gran," she had said, and my heart had swelled with pride. Not only did I now have a longed-for grandchild, it seemed this miracle child had also inherited something which had skipped a generation: a love of art, and creativity. Of course, it may just as easily have come from her father's side, but why should I not choose to believe it had come from me, and my mum?

But Ada, of course, lives in London too, and though she phones, and emails, and texts her gran, her life is busy and full, just as it should be.

So, with both children long since having left home, and my grandchild equally remote, it has been a long time since I have been needed in any practical way. And I suppose a large part of my sense of purpose has eroded. But for a long time, I still had Maudie. A friend for life. Only she hadn't been for life, as it turned out. And she had gone and died; six years ago now, but I miss her every day.

***

I have found as I've got older that I've been lucky with my health. So it's not so much a physical restraint holding me back as a lack of vigour. A deficiency in enthusiasm. Most days, I find myself more often than not in my front room, watching this small segment of the world from my window. The sea is a tantalising, sparkling, sapphire tease. Reminding me what I am missing. But I cannot imagine stripping off in the broad daylight, in front of so many strangers, revealing my papery skin and my prominent blue veins.

Sometimes, if I feel like it, I will go to the club. See the familiar faces. Hear the familiar words. But I'm still not ready to submit to that side of old age. I doubt I ever will be. The moaning, the exclamations about modern youth, and mobile phones, and video games. As if we lived in a perfect world when we were younger. As though we were perfect ourselves. Those conversations take it out of me.

And so I find myself stuck between a rock and a hard place. I am old, and will almost-happily admit it. I am knocking on ninety, for goodness' sake. But my mind will not rest, will not cave in to the comfortable acceptance of age. I want interesting, lively conversation. About politics, and art, and books. I do not want to hear day after day about the weather, or the number of tourists clogging up the town, or the terrible reliance of young people on technology. Or the Saltings – the bloody Saltings! – and the effect that it will have on the town. Not to mention the many, many health complaints, which, though no doubt real, are tiresome; the focus on them does nobody any good. Have my counterparts in fact always been like this, and it's only now, with so little to occupy their time and their minds, that it's really beginning to show?

1939

During that first year in Cornwall, or at least the first few months, Elise had hated it a lot of the time. Tregynon Manor was not so different to Whiteley Hall, with the advantage of a view that took in the land sweeping down towards the sea. There were the same austere dark wooden hallways and painted portraits of previous occupants, which to many of the girls could have been interchangeable with those at Whiteley Hall and nobody would have noticed the difference. The open aspect of the place meant that when the weather was bad, which seemed to be often, the windows shook, and there was talk of ghosts and shipwrecks, which chilled Elise to the bone. Not that she ever let on. She knew that to show weakness would be a mistake. When the summer holidays came around, some of the girls went home to their families, but most stayed on. Away from their families, away from the bombs.

Elise had been one of these girls, who was not allowed home. Annabel wrote to her weekly and it seemed she did not try to protect her daughter from the truth – Elise felt she had a full picture of the bombs raining down on her home city, streets crumbling and houses falling to their knees. Neighbours, friends, and occasionally relatives, caught up in it all. She kept a note in the back of her diary, of souls she should pray for each night. It was only when she was an adult herself, and learning more of the war, that she realised what a sanitised version Annabel had in fact shared with her. People had died, Elise had known that, but she knew none of the horrors and gruesomeness of these deaths. She had little experience of the true nature of war-torn London, having left before the Blitz began. From her quiet four-bed dorm, despite all the talk and worry of the girls and the staff, it seemed remote and unreal. Like one of the ghost stories Miriam Roberts enjoyed telling the younger girls, it was almost thrilling to think of the excitement that they were no doubt missing out on, exiled as they were to this quiet county by the sea.

As the war went on, it turned out that Cornwall was not as far removed from it all as had been expected. There was a 'mini blitz' over Bodmin one night in 1942, and many bombs rained down on Truro, Penzance and Falmouth. In quiet little Praa Sands, a Sunderland flying boat (who could imagine such a thing?) was forced to crash-land after the crew had kept it flying for 300 miles after being shot at by German fighter planes in the Bay of Biscay. Nowhere was safe, or untouched by the war, but the school staff knew that they were still far safer in this south-west corner of England than if they had remained at home.

Most of the days were spent at the manor-turned-school. A bell had been installed, and it was by this that the girls kept to their routine. Wake up. Breakfast. Lessons begin. Lunchtime. Free time. Lessons. Sports. Prep time. Teatime. Free time. Bed.

On Saturdays, there were no afternoon lessons, but Miss Forbes had decided that while the oldest girls were free to go into town in pairs, the younger ones should practise for an end-of-year play.

A Midsummer's Night Dream.

It's an excellent idea, Annabel wrote to Elise, who had voiced her consternation at this in a previous letter, and her sense of injustice at being kept in school, learning, while the older girls were free. *Just think of the skills you can gain in a play. If you don't want to act, you can create the sets. And I hope that I might be able to come for the end of term. I would love to see the play for myself. I want you to make me proud.*

Making her mother proud was Elise's main driving force, as Annabel well knew. So, reluctantly, Elise tried out for the part of Titania, queen of the fairies, and was put out once more when Miss Forbes cast her as Robin Goodfellow, or Puck – a mischievous sprite.

The teacher did her best to explain to Elise her choice, keeping her back that afternoon: "Puck holds everything together. He's not malicious. He's just got a sense of fun, like you, Elise. Do you really want to be queen of the fairies?"

Elise had shrugged slightly, but remembered her manners. "No, I suppose not, thank you, Miss Forbes."

"Good girl. Now, go and get washed before dinner."

Shoulders drooping, Elise had left the room. She had wanted to be the queen of the fairies, very much. Despite what Miss Forbes had told her, it seemed obvious that Titania was the best part. The most glamourous. To rub salt in her wound, it was Imogen who was cast as Titania, and she had no problem making sure everybody knew it.

Violet had been given the part of Peter Quince, the leader of the players, and was just relieved not to have been cast as Bottom (that honour was awarded to Gladys Matthews – a robust and good-natured girl who had accepted the role with enthusiasm).

"You know Puck gets to end the play?" Violet said quietly to Elise at dinner, as they tried to ignore Imogen's boasting at the next table.

"No," Elise said.

"He's one of Father's favourite characters," Violet told her. Violet's father was a professor of English at one of the London universities. "Father says that Robin Goodfellow is not just a character Shakespeare invented but he's renowned in English folklore. He's thought to be the son of Oberon – you know, the king of the fairies. But not in *A Midsummer Night's Dream*. Oberon just uses him to try and fix the mix-up, with the lovers."

How did Violet know so much, and speak so much like a grown-up? Elise had just nodded, thinking she really needed to read the text in full. And that night she did – and saw just how key a part Puck played in the story. And those words, at the end of the play. Suddenly, she wasn't disappointed, but incredibly nervous – and also flattered. It felt like the whole play hinged on her. She determined then and there to learn the script – the whole script – off by heart.

Sundays were the days when the whole school would walk into town to the church, where Father Nicholls had reserved pews especially for the girls. These pews were to the side of the central nave of the church, and a few rows back, but nevertheless it had seemed to Elise that some of the local people weren't best pleased at these young upstarts, *incomers*, being given these seats.

The first service they attended, Father Nicholls had welcomed the girls and their teachers: "And if you are wondering who this influx of fine young ladies is, to my left, these are the girls of Whiteley School for Girls, near London, who will be staying in our town for the duration of the war, which we pray will not be long. Not," he continued, smiling, "that you are not very welcome here, girls. And your teachers, too."

Elise thought Father Nicholls was very nice, and on Thursdays he would come to the manor house to teach the girls religious education, then he would stay on to share the evening meal with them all. Elise heard Imogen say that Father Nicholls was good looking. Wasn't it wrong to think of a vicar that way?

It definitely seemed like a different atmosphere on Thursday evenings, and Elise noticed that even the teachers seemed more cheerful on these days.

She didn't mind church, but she would spend each service counting down the minutes until they could leave, when, come rain or shine, Miss Forbes would lead them on a walk to the beach. It had been so alien to Elise at first, and many of the other girls, too. Just a handful had been on family holidays to the seaside before. For most, the sensation of walking on sand was a novelty. It was not like mud, but it was damp and cloying where the tide had been, sticking to shoes and somehow even making its way inside socks and underwear. How was that possible?

Sunday nights were also bath nights, and floors and bathtubs became coated with a fine layer of sand, which crunched underfoot and stuck to the skin once more. It was impossible to get rid of and even after a bath, when Elise was in her nightgown and wriggling into bed, sure enough it was there as well, prickling her skin ever-so-slightly uncomfortably, but also bringing to mind happy memories of the day's walk.

For she loved those walks, more than any other part of her week. And when she learned Annabel was coming to visit at the end of term, as promised, she longed to take her mother there. Had Annabel ever been to the seaside before? Elise had no idea. She had never spoken of it if she had. And surely, if she had, she would not have kept such a thing secret from her daughter, or deprived her of the experience?

Even on the coldest, greyest, and mistiest of days, Elise loved being by the sea. She might have to walk with a partner, and she might have to keep a hand on her skirts to save them blowing around her legs (revealing far too much skin than was appropriate, so the girls were repeatedly told), but despite these restrictions, she felt a little less trapped than she did in school.

It was something to do with the strength of the wind, and the wildness of the sea. The vast expanse of the beach. She wanted to run, across the sand and along the shore, but that would never be permitted. When she was old enough to come out of school on Saturday afternoons, she would come to the beach, she thought. But that was a long way off, and she hoped that the war would long be over by then.

Elise

"Hi, Elise!" the ever-enthusiastic Sarah greets me at the door to the club. Caring the Community, some bright spark had called it. A terrible name, but it had stuck. "We haven't seen you for a while. Have you been keeping OK?"

'Keeping OK.' That's one of those things they say to you when you're getting older. *When you're old*, I remind myself. When does anybody ask a twenty-year-old if they're *keeping ok*? Still, Sarah's one of the good ones. She's a lovely woman who not only runs this club, voluntarily, but is also involved in the town's youth club, and Girl Guides. I remember Sarah's mother, who died well before her time. Cancer. Oh god, why do I always start to think of death when I get to the club?

"I've been fine, thanks." I smile and shrug off my coat, hanging it up before Sarah has a chance to help me. It is my firm belief that the more I do for myself, no matter how small, the younger in outlook, and more independent, I will stay.

Inside the hall, there are a few tables laid out higgledy-piggledy, circled by chairs, which are occupied for the most part by my ageing compatriots. Looking around, I know everyone here, and I know that I have a good ten or fifteen years on some of them. It's a bit stuffy inside today, as the aged heating system and steam from the hot water urn clouds the high-level windows, and I make my way to the serving hatch, greeting people as I go.

"I'll come and sit with you in a minute," I tell Bill, a mischievous man some years my junior; he had still been at school when Davey had died – I'd been widowed while he was still wearing short trousers, but now we are on an even footing, and he's one of the people here I enjoy spending time with.

"What can I get you?" The woman behind the counter seems to sense my presence before she's turned round to see me. "Oh, hello," she says, as though she knows me.

"Hello," I am surprised to see it's the very same woman I've been observing passing my house with her daughter each day. "I'm Elise."

"I'm sure I recognise you," the woman smiles. "Although I don't know where from. I'm Maggie. I've started helping out here. Just till I get a new job. Although to be honest I'd rather just carry on doing this." She grins and pushes her dark fringe from her eyes.

"Serving up tea and coffee to us oldies? I'm sure you can find something a bit more elevating than that," I return her smile. Sometimes, I feel like my own is a bit rusty. It's like your voice. If you don't use it enough, it can dry up and feel unfamiliar.

"Don't underestimate it," Maggie says. "It's nice to be appreciated, I can assure you."

"Ah, yes…" I want to mention Maggie's daughter, and how I understand that offspring can be the last to make you feel appreciated, but then my cover will be blown, and it will be obvious that I've been watching Maggie. Which could be a bit creepy. "I know what you mean," I finish lamely.

"Tea or coffee?" Maggie asks brightly.

"I'll have a tea, please. Milk, no sugar. Thank you."

Maggie furnishes me with a drink, and the ubiquitous saucer bearing a custard cream and a Bourbon biscuit. I have never liked Bourbons, but I know Bill will wolf it down. He'd eat anything, that man.

"Thank you, Maggie." I make my way to my friend, who is waiting impatiently, and has been joined by a couple of the other men in the group.

Arthur is deftly shuffling a pack of cards. "Whist?" he asks as I take my seat at the table.

"Perfect." I enjoy a good card game. It keeps my brain ticking, and I particularly relish beating the men here, who, to be fair, happily accept my presence at their table.

Today, though, it seems my mind is only half on the game, as I am also watching Maggie. She's just as I had thought she would be; smiling, positive and friendly. And there is none of the 'how are you keeping' with her. She talks to all us oldies like we're normal people. Which, of course, we are. Most of us, at least.

One of my pet peeves is older people being described as 'sweet', or talked to as if we're children. We're the furthest from children that it is possible to be. Of course, sometimes there are the fallen ones. When bodies and minds fail and they need looking after, and they somehow do seem to revert to childlike selves. Sinking into care homes and hospices as the waters of their real lives – their vivid, vibrant, lucid lives – close over their heads. It hasn't happened to me yet, and I am very grateful for that, but I know it still could.

I will fight that fate tooth and nail, but I know it's not a matter of choice.

Maggie notices me watching and casts an open smile my way. I smile back and return to my card game. It won't do to let the men win.

The hour-and-a-half passes quickly and soon enough I'm on my way back home, accompanied part of the way by Sylvia, who lives at the same side of town.

"Do you know that Maggie, then?" Sylvia asks me.

"No, not really. I do recognise her. I think she passes by my place when she's taking her daughter to school."

"Oh, yes, that girl. She's in the same class as Mabel's Courtney. A bit of an oddball, apparently. Always wants to play with the boys."

"Oh." So, while poor Maggie was smilingly handing out drinks and washing cups for these old buggers, they'd been snidely talking about her little girl. "Well, nothing wrong with that. Little girls can be nasty sometimes. Maybe boys are more uncomplicated," I say, sharply. "And Maggie seems a nice young woman, and she's giving up her time to help us out, so maybe we should stop gossiping about her ten-year-old daughter, eh?"

Sylvia's cheeks flush. She opens her mouth but seems to decide against whatever it is she was going to say. She's a nice woman herself, though, really, and I have no wish to offend her.

"She looks a bit like your Louisa, I thought," Sylvia offers by way of, if not an apology, a conciliation.

"Yes, do you know what, I hadn't thought of that." Maggie and Louisa do share the same kind of colouring – dark hair, dark eyes, and lightly tanned skin – Louisa's over-winter tan is maintained carefully by way of regular subtle spray tans, however, whereas Maggie's is more likely a product of the wind and the regularly cold but sunny days.

"Now, how are those grandkids of yours?" I ask, and my friend is soon at ease again, telling me all about her oldest, who's at university in Bath, and the youngest, who's only just started primary school. At the top of my road, we part ways, on as good terms as ever.

I walk slowly down the steep path towards home, ready for a sandwich and a rest. Not because the club has tired me out, but because I have a late night ahead.

The afternoon drifts by in a pleasant haze. I take a cup of tea and my book up to my room, lying down on the bed. I used to think this might be akin to giving up, but I've always benefitted from a rest after lunch – even in my younger days. I remember when Laurie was a baby; the sheer joy of those post-lunch naps. He would slumber merrily, for a good hour or two, and I – free, or at least as free as I was ever going to be, for just this little wedge of time – would take the chance to rest and recuperate.

In the winter, sitting on my chair by the fire. Never Davey's, even though he wasn't there to see. I wouldn't have wanted to sit in his chair. I wanted as little as possible to do with that man.

In the spring, I would have Laurie's pram outside in the garden, and I would sit watching the washing on the line, as it danced to the tune of the wind from the sea. I'd notice the green shoots peering out of the earth, and tiny, delicate flower heads, which were always a welcome sight. And if I stood in the right spot, just by the front of the row of cottages, I could see the sea. At all times, I could hear it, attention-seeker that it is.

Ours was the last cottage on the row, and had a pleasingly larger garden, where I grew potatoes and onions and carrots. The garden adjoined the coastal path, which would take me down to town, but which was impossible with the pram. Instead, on market day and Sundays, I would have to follow the narrow, careworn road, the pram bumping along in front of me, Laurie gurgling and giggling to accompany each bounce. He had been a really happy, bonny baby, with a smile for everyone. Davey was proud of him because he was a boy. His lad. Set to follow in his footsteps.

Not if I had anything to do with it.

The walk down to town on the road was twice as long as along the coastal path. The walk back, all uphill, was twice as long again. It was hard work, pushing a pram and carrying supplies, but I suppose it kept me fit and strong. I had hoped against hope that I wouldn't get pregnant again, because god knew how I'd manage, although my neighbour, Marie, was always offering to help mind the baby. But I didn't want to be apart from Laurie. On edge all the time, I needed the warm, physical reassurance of him close by, to know that he was alright.

After Davey had died, I'd been able to move into town, to the house where I live now, and life had become brighter.

I must have dozed off, as I had expected I might, but not before finishing my tea. I wake with my book resting open on my chest, and a full bladder. But I make myself wait, just a moment, to listen. My ever-open window allows access to the sounds of the town. It's quiet, out of season, with the occasional bus passing by, and the ever-present gulls making their usual racket. The steady crash of waves onto the rocks, and the chattering sparrows twittering away in the overgrown shrubbery of a neighbouring garden.

But I can't wait too long, and I emit an all-too-familiar groan as I slowly rouse myself and edge my legs off the bed. It just takes a little longer to warm up these days, for my muscles to remember their manners. I make the short trip to the tiny bathroom, letting my fingers trail across what had been Louisa's bedroom door. Down two small steps to the bathroom on the left, next to Laurie's bedroom at the back. Both their rooms are clean and fresh, ready for guests, although these are far fewer and further between than they used to be. Still, I am looking forward to the summer, when Ada and one of her friends are coming to stay. They did the same last year – spreading the floors with sand, their trendy shampoos and body sprays scenting the air, and their young, happy voices and laughter filling the house.

"Use it as a base," I had urged them and so they had, although always considerately. They would swim and surf and have nights out on the town. In the afternoons, they'd have a siesta, which I have meant to start calling my afternoon naps. It sounds so much more invigorating and sophisticated. When they woke, they would shower, then go down the shops, coming back with their arms full of organic vegetables and fresh-baked bread, cooking up all sorts of mouth-wateringly spicy dishes to share with me. I did not have to cook once while they were here. And Ada's friend, Clara, had been an absolute pleasure. Those two girls never stop talking and laughing. It made me think of my own young friendship with Maudie, which had not been so different at first. Until I started going out with Davey, which changed everything.

Nights are still swooping in quite early, which means I do not have too long to wait for the comforting veil of darkness, although I do usually find it prudent to hang on until pub closing time, missing the few stragglers who might be stumbling through the streets. I eat late, and watch an episode of some new detective programme Louisa recommended. It's pretty dark; maybe that makes it realistic, but it also makes it hard to take in some ways. Is there any need for the level of graphic detail portrayed, really? But I'm not scared, or squeamish. My generation have seen far, far worse, which people often seem to forget. My mind darts to my mum, in London for the war, and the sights she must have seen but kept to herself. Yet for all she tried to shield me, I haven't gone through life unscathed. Maybe nobody does. And by the time my moment had come, my mum had long since died. I sometimes imagine that she was watching me, wherever she might be; wincing, or even crying, for what was happening to her daughter.

At half-past eleven, I am pulling on my coat and warm, waterproof boots. I pick up the rucksack which Ada kindly left for me, sling it onto my shoulder, then gently open my back door and peer along Godolphin Terrace. Curtains are shut along the row, and there are lights on in some of the upstairs windows. I stop, and listen. I can hear nothing but for the sea, and a car somewhere along one of the back roads. I close the back door gently behind me, not bothering to lock it. Another habit of the past, which Louisa disapproves of, but Ada thinks is 'cool'.

I take soft-footed steps across to the gate and open it, walking carefully down the alleyway and out into the night. Under cover of darkness, I cross the road, and walk through the station car park. A couple are sharing a kiss under a lamp-post. I smile to myself and continue walking. They won't notice me.

I take the steep steps down, carefully holding on to the handrail. I know I am perfectly capable and nimble for my age, but it wouldn't do to take a false step. My body would not cope well with a fall, and I would be nimble and capable no more.

My pace quickening as I move onto the slope, I can feel my heart rate increasing, and the welcoming breeze on my face, carrying echoes of songs from the deep, forgotten dreams, and memories of other nights, long ago. The voice of the sea is strong and true now.

There.

I step off the concrete onto the soft sands. Look left and right. Just as I had hoped. There is not another soul about. The beach, and the night, are mine.

1941

As if the big wide world wasn't changing enough, when Elise was twelve, her own smaller world was rocked to its core.

"Elise, can you come with me?" Miss Forbes had come to find her one evening, just as she was preparing for bed. Pale-faced, the teacher shot a look at Matron, who stood back to let the girl pass. The concern on the faces of the two women was not missed by Elise. She knew it could be only one thing.

Unless... unless... she grasped for some other explanation. Had her scholarship been withdrawn? Was she in trouble for something? She could think of nothing she had done, but the possibility that she was going to be unfairly disciplined was infinitely more attractive than that other reality. She walked, dreamlike, after Miss Forbes, who didn't say anything more. She was, in fact, shocked and dismayed herself, but Elise could not be expected to know that.

Miss Hazlehurst was sitting in her study. All of the teachers, being single women with no children, had moved with the school to Cornwall. It might be said that it was suiting some of them very well. With suntans and bright eyes, it seemed the sea air had breathed some extra life into them. Miss Hazlehurst, who appeared ancient to the girls, was in fact only in her fifties, and was enjoying life on the coast very much indeed. Today, though, her face looked pale.

"Elise," she smiled kindly. "Do take a seat."

Elise did as she was told, and swallowed. Her whole body was tingling, and it felt like her mind was detaching from her physical being. Miss Forbes, instead of sitting on the other side of the desk, pulled up a chair next to her. This was it, then. The thing Elise had feared most.

"I have bad news, I'm afraid, my dear," Miss Hazlehurst began.

Elise said nothing.

"It concerns your mother."

A brief, fleeting moment, when the mention of Annabel in such a way suggested she might still be alive. 'Your mother'. It implied the present tense. That Elise did still have a mother.

"There was another bombing raid on London, two nights ago, near your house. From what we have been told, your mother was on her way to work, but she... she..." Miss Hazlehurst took a deep breath. The girl in front of her was composed but ashen-faced. "Elise, your mother died in the raid. I'm so sorry to tell you. So very, very sorry."

It had happened. There was no present tense. Annabel was now past.

Annabel has, Annabel will, Annabel is.

Annabel had, Annabel would, Annabel was.

Not Annabel, Elise thought. *Mummy.* Mummy. And with the thought of that name, the tears came.

"Mummy," she whispered, and Miss Forbes' arms were around her.

"I'm so sorry," she said. "So sorry." And she held Elise close and rocked the girl, the teacher's own tears falling, too.

Miss Hazlehurst sat, and watched. Composed and yet defeated. This war. It was taking the best of the nation, and withering souls. Sucking out positivity and replacing it with a dim acceptance. Every day came news of bombs falling, and not just in London. Bristol, Liverpool, Hull, Birmingham, Manchester, Cardiff, Clydebank, Belfast, Sheffield.

And now this poor girl's mother. A nurse. A lovely young woman. Miss Hazlehurst remembered the pride on her face during Elise's interview. Then the day Elise started.

Overseeing the usual comings and goings of the first day of term, she had watched from the steps as the woman had left her daughter behind. Most girls had come in family cars, but Elise and her mother had come by train. They had been driven from the station to the school by Mr Brownlow, the local grocer, who would also act as a taxi service when required. It would appear that this young woman could only afford the ride one way, however, and would be walking the two miles back to the station.

It was a different life for the scholarship girls. And what about their parents? These girls were needed at home. They were useful, in helping to run the home, look after younger siblings. Their loss would be felt in more way than one. In the Morgans' case, there was only one parent. There were no siblings. So the widowed mother was walking home, into a life alone. The way her shoulders drooped once she thought she was out of sight, and her head fell. The headmistress had wanted to go after her, to tell her they would look after her girl, but she knew that her role was to stay strong and stable and be seen by all – girls and parents alike. As luck had it, Miss Forbes was available, and she went to Elise's mother. Miss Hazlehurst watched the English teacher briefly put a hand on the mother's shoulder but then, accosted by Imogen Lee's father, her attention was ushered elsewhere. When she looked back, there was no sign of Mrs Morgan, or of her member of staff.

Now, little Elise Morgan sat in her office, in a state of abject grief. The headmistress had been pleased that the tears had come. She had seen before girls in a state of shock, of mute acceptance. It wasn't healthy. Here, although she would take away this misery if she possibly could, was a girl who was feeling it alright. And this was just the beginning. The grief would last a lifetime. And then there were practical concerns. The scholarship. The end of the war – because surely it would end one day, wouldn't it? This girl now had no home to go to. And in the meantime, nobody to send her parcels or letters. She was alone.

"Miss Forbes, perhaps you'd like to take Elise back to her room? Where she might be more comfortable?"

Miss Forbes looked at Miss Hazlehurst. She saw the example being set and she too pulled herself upright. She wiped the tears from her face and put her hands on the girl's shoulders. "Elise?"

The girl looked at the teacher.

"We'll go upstairs, shall we? Back to your room. Back to Violet, too. I know she'll want to know what's happened."

Violet Wetherbourne, Miss Hazlehurst thought with satisfaction, was just the kind of friend Elise needed.

Elise nodded and allowed herself to be shepherded from the room. The teacher and the headmistress shared a brief look and, when the door was closed, Miss Hazlehurst allowed herself a little weakness. Just for a few moments. She let her head rest in her hands, massaging her temples. Now was not the time for tears. This was just another cruel blow in this world which was full of them. Tears would not help the girl, but if there was one thing Miss Hazlehurst knew, it was that Whiteley School had never let a girl down yet. She pulled her shoulders back, took a deep breath, let it out slowly, and sat strong and straight once more.

Upstairs, Violet was waiting in her nightdress, tucked under the thin covers. Summer was rapidly galloping in, and the nights were becoming sticky and humid. She looked up as Miss Forbes entered, gently guiding Elise by the hand.

"May I tell Violet?" The teacher sought Elise's permission. The girl nodded.

"I'm afraid Elise has had some terrible news, Violet. Her mother has... has died. From a bomb. In London."

"Oh." Violet felt like she had been punched in the stomach. It wasn't her own mother. She had never even met Mrs Morgan. But she felt shocked, and sick, and angry. So god only knew how Elise felt. She pushed her covers back and went straight to her friend, putting her arms around her. Gently, she guided Elise's head to her shoulder. "Oh, Elise. I am sorry. I am so sorry."

Miss Forbes stood back, pleased at least that Elise's friend here was so very mature and steady. "Will you take care of her tonight, Violet?"

"Of course."

"Good. Then I'll leave you two girls to it, but I will make sure Matron comes to see you soon, with something to help you sleep, Elise. And do not hesitate to ask for me if you need me. Alright?"

"Thank you, Miss Forbes," said Violet, leading Elise to the bed, where they could sit next to each other. Elise went obediently, her mind elsewhere anyway. The sight broke Miss Forbes' heart.

Angela Forbes shut the door behind her and sought out Matron, telling her the news. Then she hurried away to her room, to cry her own private tears.

Elise

It's a late start to the day, as it always is after one of my night-time rambles. Rambling in the sense of walking, but also in the sense of the trains of thoughts which rattle through my head. Memories, mostly, but these days mixed in with thoughts of the future; if I am honest, how many days, weeks, months, years lie ahead of me. I don't mind, really; I know I have been fortunate to have survived, when so many of my friends and peers have fallen, some way too young. Like my mum, and the millions of people who died in that war. And all the wars since, and before.

I remember how Angela Forbes had told me that despite all the ills of war – and at this point we'd had no idea about the concentration camps – some good would come.

"For women," she had exclaimed. I can see her face now; excitement and optimism written all over it. "We've been able to show just what we are capable of. There can be no going back now."

She'd been hopeful of equality, but of course it hadn't worked like that. The expectation of the roles women must play, and just what we are capable of, is a long, complex thing to untangle. The war may have pulled out a knot or two, but there is clearly still so much more to be done.

So, yes, ramblings. I let my feet and my mind take me where they wish, like I am a passenger along for the ride. But the following morning, I can feel it in my aching muscles. The after-effect of the steps and the steep slopes either end of the beach. But it isn't altogether unpleasant; the achiness a reminder of my ability to still climb those slopes, and get about freely. Another example of my good fortune. I am relatively strong and fit, and I intend to stay that way for as long as I am alive.

A couple of pieces of toast, from the loaf I made yesterday – or was it the day before that? A strong cup of coffee (half a teaspoon of sugar and a drop of cream to soften the blow). A shower and hair-wash... then what? This is the problem. The days. Evenings seem to flow easily, somehow filling themselves, so that even if I have planned on an early night, I will find myself only getting up to bed at eleven, and then reading, and perhaps falling asleep before midnight. Days, though, are a different matter.

I take a seat in my chair by the window, looking out. Watching the cars and the passers-by. Letting my mind wander again. Then, the phone. At this time of day? I almost can't be bothered to get up; it will almost certainly be a cold caller. But it's something to do, at least.

Louisa

My daughter's name shocks and delights me. Shouldn't she be at work now? Louisa never calls during the day, unless it's a weekend. Suddenly, my delight turns to worry. Is something wrong?

"Hello? Love?"

"Hi, Mum." The sound of traffic is clear behind Louisa's strong voice. A siren. The beep of a horn. I am glad not to live in London. I find it hard to believe that I ever did.

"Hi, Louisa. How are you?" I know better than to ask if everything is alright; to manifest my fear of something terrible happening to my children.

"I'm fine, Mum. Are you?"

"Yes, thanks. A bit tired today, you know."

"Well, make sure you rest a bit, then."

"It's all I ever do!" I laugh. "Now, aren't you meant to be at work?"

"Yes, I am, I've just stepped out for a bit. It's a beautiful day."

This is out of character.

Louisa continues, "I just wanted to see how you are, Mum. And to let you know I'm coming to Cornwall in a few weeks."

"Really?" *Play it down, Elise.* My heart is jumping for joy.

"Yes, I thought... I thought maybe we could spend some time together. You know, I might come for a week. Maybe more."

"OK..." I am worried again. "Is everything OK?" I ask tentatively, aware I could get shouted at.

But Louisa just laughs. "Yes, Mum, everything's fine. I'm fine. I just... I know we haven't spent a lot of time together lately, and I miss you, and I miss Cornwall, I suppose. It's been hard at work lately and I can't think of anywhere I'd rather be."

"Well, my love, you know you're welcome any time, and you know I'd love to see you." I am starting to breathe normally again. "Your room's always ready for you. Well, unless Ada's visiting, of course!"

"Oh thanks, Mum, but I think I'll stay in the hotel."

"Oh." That's more like it. I should have known Louisa would prefer to stay at Tregynon than spend a week in her childhood bedroom. Then again, it is a rare break for her. She deserves to spoil herself.

"You don't mind, do you?"

"No, no, of course I don't." And I find that, actually, I really don't mind. My daughter is coming home. Just for a week. But – a whole week!

Hotel or not, I can't help but feel delighted.

1945

At first, the girls had thought they might be in Cornwall for a handful of months.

"Home next summer, eh girls?" Mrs Bishop, the cook, would say smilingly. She was a local woman, whose three boys had all gone off to fight. Despite the worry she must have been experiencing, she always had a smile and a pleasant word.

It was impossible to imagine anything else, and entirely unthinkable that it might be over six years before the Whiteley School for Girls returned to its original premises. By then, the numbers had dwindled, as some girls had grown up and shuffled out of the education system, and there was no new intake. There could not be, really, until things returned to normal.

Elise had spent a third of her life in Cornwall, and at nearly sixteen was about ready to leave school herself. When she looked back to that train journey, when she was not yet ten years old, it felt like looking at a different world. The world had changed of course, in those years, and the extent to which it had changed had been nowhere near fully revealed. And Elise's world had changed, too. She had left London a child and was ready to return a young woman. Her body had changed, as much as her manners and her interests.

She and Violet were now old enough to walk out to town themselves, and attend the odd dance. They loved these dances, although often felt themselves a little on the edge of things. The local girls would stare at them, and whisper amongst themselves. Elise knew she was deemed a toff, for her place at a prestigious girls' school, though her background was really no different from these girls'. But no matter her background, her education had been different, and that was sometimes telling.

It also did not help that some of the local boys had taken quite an interest in Elise. Violet was not bothered, or at least claimed not to be. While she loved the dances, and the independence she and Elise had been allowed, she was equally at home with her books and in the science lab. She seemed not to have any interest in the boys; just the dancing. Elise was a bit different.

There was one boy in particular who had caught her eye. She often noticed him looking at her, and sometimes he'd give her a cheeky grin, while she was being whisked around the floor by one of his friends. She did not smile back, or she tried not to, anyway.

So, on a Saturday afternoon, Elise and Violet would ready themselves for the dances. It took some creativity not to look exactly the same every week, with their limited clothing and lack of make-up.

***

When the war had actually, finally, ended, there were such celebrations. It was a moment of pure joy. Despite the huge loss of life and the devastation. Cornwall had not escaped unscathed, despite having been deemed a suitable place for evacuees. Penzance had suffered badly, with over eight hundred bombs dropped upon it. The whole landscape had changed, with pill boxes and US Army camps; barbed wire defences on the beaches, and radar stations dotted around the county.

The social topography had changed, too, with women so

much more involved in life outside the home. Even in Cornwall, which seemed a little detached from the progressive towns and cities upcountry, as the locals called it, there were signs. There were young female ATS everywhere. There were also Black American soldiers, who were the topic of many a conversation but who by and large were as welcome as all the other GIs (i.e. welcome to a point, as long as they steered clear of the local women – which was not always the case). Elise hoped fervently that these little indications of progress, and steps towards equality, were here to stay.

There was no thought that day of the years of deprivation still to come. Right then, the nightmare was over, and the sense of joy and relief was tangible.

The little Cornish town was no exception, and Elise and Violet were lost in the crowds, and excitement, as it seemed that all of the townsfolk were out that day. Down at the harbour, the local band were playing. The fishing fleet did not leave harbour. It was a suitably warm, sunny day, and there had been time to plan ahead for this once-in-a-lifetime celebration, as rumours of the war's end had been rife for some time.

Elise and Violet had been walking towards town when they heard a cry from down the hill. An unforgettable voice, which decades later Elise could still summon to her mind: "The war is over! They've surrendered! Jerry's given in!"

There were answering shouts and cries and, shortly after, the church bells began to peal. An engine resting at the station started sounding its whistle and the air somehow seemed to fill with voices lifting up and an excitement almost impossible to describe.

The girls hurried on, finding the streets filling with people, smiling and laughing and congratulating each other. There were women hugging, and a small toddler crying, bemused and confused by the sheer number of people and the din they were making.

From an open window came loud music – *Knees Up Mother Brown*, the *Lambeth Walk*, and the *Hokey Cokey*. A line of people formed, snaking along the street. Elise and Violet knew they should have been going back to school, but it was impossible to leave and when, eventually, they returned, the staff were too happy and relieved themselves to think of any form of discipline. It was a day, and a night, to remember, and Elise had found herself wishing it might never end.

Elise

After lunch, I go into my garden for a while. It is small;
little more than a yard, really, with a square of lawn at
the back, which I purchased from the council back in the
seventies. My two raised beds run along the side. This
year, in one of the beds I am trying the 'three sisters'
(sweetcorn, beans and squash), although I am not
convinced there's enough space for the sweetcorn. Still, I
like the idea of the extravagant-looking plants and hope
they will be relatively low maintenance. The other bed
houses tomatoes, lettuce and cucumber.

My garden is a source of great pleasure, although it is
far smaller than the one I had at the house where we
lived with Davey. I do miss that garden, if nothing else
about that place, and remember fondly those days with
the washing blowing eagerly in the breeze that climbed
and crept over the cliffs – and the children as babies,
sleeping soundly up there, tucked safe inside a pram, but
open to the elements. When Laurie was a boy and Louisa
was a baby, he would sit watching the sea birds, using a
pair of binoculars that had belonged to Davey's dad.
Davey's mum had given them to Laurie, after her
husband had died. I would watch Laurie in turn, my
heart swelling with joy and pride at the sight of his
earnest little face. There were some happy times, until
Davey came home.

I pull a few little weeds from the soil and grit my teeth at the thought of my husband. What would my mum have thought of him, if they'd ever had the chance to meet? Would she have seen through him? Warned me? But I know that without him, there would be no Louisa or Laurie. No Ada. That would never do.

A sharp, shocked cry breaks my chain of thought. It sounds like a child. I can hear a woman's voice comforting, and then more crying. Deep, gut-wrenching sobs. It sounds like they're out on the street. I open the wooden garden gate. There is a cool, dark passageway to the right, which leads from my back garden to the road, and a path to the left that takes a bend to run along behind the other houses in the terrace and eventually meets up with the road again.

Looking right, I can see Maggie, stooped over her sobbing daughter.

"Hello," I call, "are you alright?" Although I can see that they're not.

"Oh," Maggie says, looking round and squinting to see who has addressed her. Her cheeks are flushed, and she looks harassed. She identifies me despite the shadows of the alleyway. "Oh," she says again, and manages a smile. "Hello. Yes, it's just my daughter. She managed to fall over and cut her leg."

"I didn't do it on purpose," comes an indignant voice, and I suppress a smile.

"Oh dear," I say. "Can I help? Would you like to come and clean up in my house? I was just in the garden. You'd be very welcome."

"Oh no, it's OK," Maggie says. "Thank you."

"Can I see?" I ask, emerging from the passageway, my

eyes taking a moment to adjust to the change in light. I can see the girl's knees are both bleeding, and one looks a bit swollen. "Oh dear, that looks nasty," I smile at the girl. "Are you sure you don't want to just come in and clean it before you go home? It's no bother."

"Yes please," the girl says, before her mum has a chance to answer.

"Stevie!" Maggie scolds, but can't help smiling. "Well, OK then, if you're sure. Thank you. We've still got a few minutes till we get to our house, so it might be a good idea."

"Of course." I move past them to push my front door open. "Come on in." Maggie and her daughter follow obediently. "Now, take a seat, please, and let me get some warm water and a cloth. And I think I've got some nice big plasters somewhere." I smile at the girl. "What's your name, my love?"

"Stevie." The girl has stopped crying and is now looking about her, unashamedly nosy.

What does she make of my place? Probably standard old-person stuff.

"This is really kind of you," Maggie says.

"Oh, it's no bother. Believe me, I'm grateful for a break in the old routine," I say, hastily adding, "Not that I'd have wanted you to fall over, Stevie."

The girl smiles. Her face is a little puffy and red from her tears, and her right knee is swelling, too. It does look nasty.

"I'll put the kettle on too, if you'd like a cup? And some squash for you, Stevie?" Am I pushing my luck? Do they really just want to get out of here and on their way home as quickly as possible?

"Do you know what? That would be lovely," Maggie says gratefully.

I fetch a small bowl of warm water and a cloth, and my first aid kit. While Maggie performs the necessary cleaning and patching, I make us all drinks and reach for my biscuit tin. It's a pleasure to have visitors. It's been some time since I've had anyone in.

"Here we are," I say. "Now, Stevie, would you like me to put the TV on for you?"

Stevie looks at her mum, who smiles and nods. "Yes, please. Do you have CBBC? CBeebies is for babies."

"I don't know what I've got," I chuckle. "There are a lot of channels, and I only watch maybe four of them, but you're welcome to have a look. And here, put your feet up on this stool and give those legs of yours a chance to rest a bit. They've had a nasty shock."

Stevie looks delighted.

"This is really kind of you," Maggie says again.

"Not at all," I wave the thanks away. It's me who feels pathetically grateful.

"Well, thank you."

We sit at the small table, while Stevie finds her channel and tucks into her biscuits with pleasure.

"Are you from the town?" I ask Maggie, although I already know the answer. I know everyone who comes from the town. And their parents, and probably their grandparents, too.

"No, I... we... moved here about a year ago. From further north." From her accent, it's clear 'north' means further up the county, not the country.

"Oh yes?" I sense this is not a subject I should ask too much about. "And do you like it here?"

"Do you know what? I really do," Maggie's smile dimples her face, and I can't help but smile back. "It was a bit strange at first, but people have been so friendly, and Stevie's settled in really well."

I think of what Sylvia said, about the kids thinking Stevie odd for playing with the boys, but what does Sylvia know?

"It's a lovely school. Or it was in my children's day. I remember it well."

"Did you go there, too?"

"No, I didn't. I lived in London when I was a girl. Came here in the war."

"With your family?"

"No," I explain about the evacuation to Cornwall, and Maggie drinks it all in.

"Wow," she says. "I can't imagine what it must have been like. Were you very scared?"

"No, I don't think so." I cast my mind back. "I might have been worried about Mum, but she hid a lot of what was happening from me. I thought I knew, but it was only much later that I found out what life was really like in London then. I think coming here was a bit of an adventure, really. Although I did miss my mum, a lot. But I would have done, wherever the school was."

"Yes, it must be strange, living away from home at such a young age. I could never send Stevie away. I'm sorry, I don't mean your mum shouldn't have..."

"I know," I smile. "It wasn't really what Mum wanted, either, but she felt like I'd be safer, and have a top-notch education, too. She was very keen on that idea. And the school was very forward-thinking. About women's rights, and their role in the world, you know."

"Well, that sounds pretty great."

"It was, really. It was." I take a sip of my tea. "They say school days are the happiest days of your life, don't they? I don't know about that, for everyone. I don't suppose that one rule can apply, but when I think about being a child, and the simplicity of life, I can see there's some truth in it. Before responsibility, and worry, and... well, you know what it's like being an adult, and a mother. How are your legs now, Stevie?" I call across to the girl, who turns, puts her thumbs up, and returns to her programme.

"I do know what you mean," Maggie says. "I loved school; or at least I loved that time of life. We always had friends round at our house, my sister and me. And we had two dogs, and guinea pigs, and a rabbit. It was a busy house," she laughs. "My mum didn't work, or at least she didn't go out to work. I suspect in reality we all kept her busy every single day. But we had a good time." She is smiling again, her eyes not looking up as she remembers, and a slow sadness intrudes on her features. "And yes, when you get a bit older, it can become a bit less fun, can't it?"

"Sometimes," I say, "but trust me, when you've lived as long as I have, you realise there's time for more fun. Even if it sometimes feels like you might never smile again."

1947

Although the war had ended over a year earlier, many evacuees across the country were delayed in returning to their families, and the decision had been made by Miss Hazlehurst, and the girls' families, that they would stay on in Cornwall, until such a time as life seemed to bear some resemblance to normality again. There was much going on in the cities hit hardest by the German bombs. So many buildings destroyed; so many people to rehome. While the family remained away from Tregynon Manor, the school could stay, and so they did.

By the time the plans were in place to vacate the grand old building, which had come to feel so much like home to staff and children alike, Elise and Violet were approaching eighteen years old ("So we've done our job with you, girls, and you have grown into young ladies, of whom we are very proud," Miss Hazlehurst told them fondly.)

At the same time, the world had come round from the jubilation and celebrations, and the feeling of immense relief that the war was over. The hard work had begun, to put things right. Physically, and economically, and politically, the world was being rebuilt, with the hope that nothing like this would ever happen again.

What now, for the girls and women of Whiteley School? Back to homes they had not seen in years. Parents and siblings, who had become in some cases distant memories, writing letters with the same old news. For nothing much seemed to move on during the war. Sometimes brothers were conscripted, and among her schoolmates, it was not just Elise who suffered bereavement (although it was only she who found herself quite alone in the world). The thought of returning was strange for all the girls, and not necessarily welcome.

Those at Whiteley who had seen out the whole of the evacuation had become a kind of family to each other. Girls and staff alike, although the adults were careful to ensure that boundaries were never blurred.

"What are you going to do, Elise?" Violet had asked. She would be going back to her family, and had half a thought to ask if her friend could come, too.

"I don't know." It had been a recurring worry for Elise that, once the war was over, or she was too old for school – whichever came first – she had nowhere to go, and nobody to go to. Could she work at the school? She would gladly do so, and the thought was comforting.

In the end, it was Angela Forbes who had solved the problem.

"I'm staying here, Elise," she had said in her straightforward way. "Cornwall suits me. I have handed in my notice and I'm going to be working at the local primary school. I want you to stay here, too. In fact, once the family from Tregynon Manor have returned, they need a governess. It doesn't need to be a live-in position, so you can live with me. They know you are just out of school yourself, and I'm afraid the pay is not much, but it will give you a start and you will have a roof over your head."

It was stated rather than asked, almost as though Elise didn't have a choice, which she supposed she didn't, really.

"I... thank you, Miss Forbes."

Did she want to stay in Cornwall? Could she imagine

returning to London? Even if she did, where would she go? The rented flat she had shared with Annabel would not be available – even if it hadn't been razed to the ground by the Germans.

The more she thought about it, the happier the prospect became. She could keep the sea. The beaches. The clifftop walks. She remembered the city, and knew she should return, if only to visit Annabel's grave. The thought of going back long-term was scary, though. She had nothing to ground her there. She thought of her old friends. Susan, with the sparkling blue eyes. What might have had happened to them? Whether they had been evacuated, or stayed at home, her days playing out with them on the city streets felt like another lifetime. So... Cornwall it was.

"There's just one more thing," Miss Forbes had said. "When we've left the school, you can call me Angela."

That would take some getting used to.

It was hard saying goodbye to Violet, who herself was reluctant to leave, although excited at the prospect of further studies and perhaps, just maybe, if she could convince her family, university.

"I'll be the first woman from our family to get a degree," she said to Elise on one of their last Saturday outings into the little Cornish town. It was a searingly beautiful day, the sky sharp and blue overhead. And free of planes. It was still a novelty, not to always be listening out for the heavy, attention-seeking sound of oily engines filling the air.

"I know you can do it," Elise had said. "I can't say I envy you; I've had enough learning."

"We never stop learning, Elise. Whatever we're doing."

Violet's earnestness had always made Elise smile. But people could sometime mistake it for a kind of weakness. Elise knew better. Violet had seen her through that hardest of harsh winters, when Annabel was freshly dead, and Elise's dreams were filled with her. It had been a deep, physical ache that she had experienced, and waves of sickness could ambush her at any time. She had lost her appetite, and lost weight. Violet, and Miss Forbes, had kept her going. Now Violet was going, too. But Miss Forbes – Angela – was somehow here to stay.

Would it be strange, living with a teacher? No doubt.

Would it be hard, teaching somebody's children in their own home? Almost certainly. But it was a solution to her situation, which somebody had kindly found for her, and she was determined to make the best of it, while she worked out what the rest of her life might hold in store. She may not have envied Violet her years of study, but she did envy the assuredness her friend had as to what she wanted to do with her life. And she hoped very much that it all worked out – if Violet had anything to do with it, it would.

Saying goodbye on the station platform, Violet pressed a small, long box into Elise's hand.

Elise opened it, seeing a beautiful fountain pen encased in a soft green velvet.

"Your pen!" she exclaimed. This had been a gift from Violet's grandmother, and Elise knew how much her friend loved it. Her mouth dropped for a moment. "I haven't anything to give you." It was true. She had literally the clothes on her back and a couple of changes, and that was it. The scholarship had seen her through her school years and provided a little for clothing. The uniform had become a lot more flexible during the war, when it was hard to get hold of many everyday things, never mind very specific skirts, blazers, blouses, even socks and knickers. There were hand-me-downs, of course, which enabled the younger girls to look the part, or very nearly, but for older girls, there were not so many options.

The girls had become more interested in their own appearances as they'd grown up, but there was not much outside feedback, aside from the local boys, who Elise suspected were interested more because the girls from Whiteley School seemed exotic and unusual compared to those they had grown up with.

Violet hugged Elise now. "Your friendship has always been a gift," she said.

And the tears came. Elise kissed her friend on the cheek and prayed this would not be the last time they saw each other. It was impossible to know anymore, and nothing could be taken for granted.

Violet climbed aboard and Elise waved goodbye to the other girls, and the teachers who were escorting them. Some of the teachers had already left, going back to family homes with ageing parents for a brief break before returning to the original Whiteley School, where life would resume much the same as it always had been – but not quite.

Elise turned to Miss Forbes.

Angela.

"Let's go home," the teacher said.

The little house was on Godolphin Terrace, not far from the harbour. It was quite a thing, for a single woman to have procured this for herself, and it might take some time for the neighbours to get used to this very modern woman with her very modern ways, but Angela was open and friendly, and seemed to let any possible insults or slights roll off her back without making a mark.

From hushed remarks, it seemed that Angela's style of dress was one thing about her to cause some offence, much as it had been a topic of gossip amongst Whiteley parents. She told Elise that the reason she had such high-quality jackets and trousers was that they had belonged to her father, who had died some years before the war. Angela had begged her mother for his entire wardrobe, and had worked with a friend to doctor them in all kinds of clever ways to fit her smaller, more feminine figure. Nevertheless, they did lend her a masculine air, and it seemed that this stood her apart from the other women who lived in the row, who tended more towards dresses and cardigans, although this may have been more down to what was available at the time rather than outright choice.

Head held high, however, Angela would exit the house to walk to her school, or the shops with her ration book, and never fail to greet the people she passed with a bright friendly 'Good morning', or 'Lovely afternoon', and a smile. It would take the boldest of characters and the coldest of countenances to ignore her.

Elise was more sensitive but was determined to follow Angela's lead. She too would offer open smiles to their neighbours, but was shyer in her approach. She was happy to leave the food shopping to Angela, and was often up at the house for hours anyway, the Camelford-Bassetts being quite a demanding family.

It was so strange to be back at Tregynon Manor, now that it had shed its school persona and returned to being an obscenely large family home. The Camelford-Bassetts had been tucked away in the Scilly Isles for the duration of the war, and their existing governess had recently left. Elise learned from the children that there had been more than one governess over the years. After a while, she began to understand why.

But she liked the children, a lot. As one of the youngest brought down to Cornwall with Whiteley School, and as an only child, she had not much experience of children younger than herself. Charles, Edmond and Tabitha were all under the age of ten and they were eager to learn, and equally eager to have fun.

In the evenings at home, Angela and Elise worked out lesson plans together, which they could take to their respective workplaces, and Elise learned a lot from her former teacher. She was able to walk up to Tregynon prepared for the day ahead.

What she could not prepare for, however, was the weather, and sometimes she would arrive soaked to the skin. The children would laugh at her, and she'd smile, despite her shivers, but the housekeeper, a local lady called Mrs Peters, would usher her through the kitchen to dry off and warm up, and insist that the children work at the kitchen table for the morning.

"Won't their parents mind?" Elise had asked the first time.

Lord and Lady Camelford-Bassett had been very specific with their instructions, that all learning was to be done in the library. She had a feeling they would not approve of their children spending time in the kitchen in this way.

"Well, between you and me, they're so rarely here, they haven't a clue what goes on in their own home." Mrs Peters said. "She's always at her sister's, up country, and god knows where *he* is. They're better when they're not together. We might have been safe from the Germans on the Scillies, but it was like another war going on inside the house."

"Really?" Elise couldn't help being fascinated by this gossipy side of Mrs Peters.

"Oh, yes, they don't get on, don't get on at all."

"But they're married."

"Only because they have to be!" Mrs Peters laughed at Elise's naivety. "Don't you know, in their world it's all set out for them. They have to marry someone else with money, and as there's not that many about, it's not a big pool to choose from. Besides," she lowered her voice, "some say that Charles was already on his way before the betrothal."

"On his way?"

"Oh, Elise," Mrs Peters smiled kindly. "You've not seen a lot of the world, have you?"

"I was born in London," Elise protested. "The capital city."

"Yes, my love, but you were just a child when you left, not much older than Charles is now, and you've been stuck in that lovely school for the last few years. All girls and women, wasn't it?"

"Yes." It was true. Elise had very, very little experience of men and, if truth be told she found Lord Camelford-

Bassett, with his confident manner and brusque ways, close to terrifying.

"Well, you'll learn, no doubt," Mrs Peters said, a look of consternation on her face. "Though not too soon, if I have anything to do with it."

This puzzled Elise but, as the children were being ushered in by their nanny, Geraldine, who had been Lady Camelford-Bassett's own nanny ("The only one she'd allow near her children, or her husband," Mrs Peters had said knowingly), it was time for a professional front, as Angela called it.

"Good morning, children," Elise said.

"Good morning, Elise," they said together, and Tabitha ran to hug her. This was not strictly a professional way of being, but Elise couldn't help but hug the little girl back.

"Time to learn," she said, and sat the children down in their respective places, positioning herself with her back to the fire to see off any lingering dampness.

Mrs Peters was right about the Camelford-Bassetts being away most of the time and life at Tregynon was not all that different to how it had been when it was hosting the school. The place ran according to the staff. There were not so many staff, and not so many children, but there was a routine, and there were rules, and they kept life ticking along.

It was certainly a more relaxed place to be when the parents were away, and when they were home their presence in the house was tangible, whether Elise saw them or not. Sometimes, the lord would have shooting parties, which the children hated. Elise did, too.

Something about the sight of the dead birds' bodies made her stomach twist, and brought to mind imagined scenes of a bombed London, and her own beautiful mother's body. She tried very hard not to imagine what had become of Annabel, but it was hard sometimes to stop her mind from going that way.

Lord Camelford-Bassett, however, was determined that his children – or his sons, at least – would follow in his footsteps, and on Wednesday afternoons the boys were taken for riding lessons, and it was just Elise and Tabitha. Elise loved the boys, but she also loved these afternoons. She would take her young charge walking in the grounds, or sometimes down to the beach. They might collect flowers, or shells, and bring them back to the house to draw them. Elise would pull books from the shelves of the library and read to Tabitha about them.

"This is the Common Periwinkle," she would say, in a funny voice to make Tabitha laugh. But then they would write the name down, together. "This is found all over the British coast. It is a species of sea snail."

During one such session, she heard the library door open and she looked up, expecting it to be Mrs Peters, or perhaps one of the boys. But it was Lord Camelford-Bassett. He smiled at her. "Carry on," he said, and he walked over to the bookshelves, his back to Elise and Tabitha.

No word of greeting for his daughter, Elise noted, but she felt her face flush, too. And became suddenly self-conscious. But Tabitha was looking at her expectantly, seemingly unperturbed by the lack of attention from her own dad.

"So shall we have a go at drawing it?" Elise said.

"Yes please, Elise," the little girl said.

Elise carefully took two sheets of paper and set them down next to each other, the cleaned shell on a piece of cloth between them.

"See the shape of its shell. And the colours. What colour do you think it is, Tabitha?" Elise fought the urge to clear her throat. She pushed her voice to sound clear and strong.

"Brown."

"It is; it is brown, but it's not just brown, is it? Look, there are greys, and cream, and the base is white. And look at the pattern, too. Do you think you can draw that?"

"I can try."

"Me too. Let's see what we can do."

Lord Camelford-Bassett had turned to watch the lesson in progress and, as Elise raised her eyes, he smiled at her. Just a small smile, but his eyes were on hers, and it made her feel like an animal caught in a cage. There was no escape. She felt her cheeks grow hotter.

He twirled the book in his hands and said, "I'll leave you to it." Out he went, leaving Elise distinctly unsettled.

From that point on, his lordship would often make an appearance on a Wednesday afternoon. Never when Elise was with his sons, for some reason, but when they'd been shipped off to their ponies and it was just Elise and Tabitha, back from their walk and sitting in the library, in he would come. Sometimes fleetingly – "Don't mind me" – and sometimes for longer. He might seat himself in the window with a book, and every now and then would cast a glance Elise's way. At first it unnerved her, and she ended up telling Angela one evening.

"Uh-oh," said her former teacher, which alarmed Elise even further.

"What?"

"Watch out, that's all. It sounds like he's interested in you."

"Interested...?" Elise may not have had much experience with men or boys, but she had read enough books and plays to have some idea of these things. "But he's married."

Angela laughed drily. "Yes, as if that ever put a man off trying his luck. Not all men, sorry – I'm being unfair, but believe me, there are enough men out there who wouldn't let a minor detail like being married put them off trying their luck."

Elise stared into the fire. It was springtime, and she'd been living with Angela for two thirds of a year now. They'd seen their first winter through and had fallen into a companionable friendship. It no longer felt strange to use Miss Forbes' first name, and the two of them often spoke of Annabel, which was a comfort to Elise, being very keen to never forget her mum, or let her memory fade. The flames licked the blackened bricks of the chimney, and Elise could hear the rain on the windowpane. She tried to work out how to word her next question, without causing offence. Although she already knew Angela enough to realise it would take some effort to offend her.

"Have you... have you ever had this, with a man? A married man?"

"Ha! No, not me. I'm not pretty enough. And besides, I think it's plain from a mile off that I wouldn't be interested."

"Do you think that I might give the impression that I would be interested?" Elise's brow knotted in concern.

"Oh no, not at all, my dear. I didn't mean it like that. You just stand your ground. It's lucky you're living here with me, though, not a live-in like their other governesses have been."

"You know about the other governesses?"

"Some, yes. You know this town is rife with gossip. And I do believe I'm gaining people's trust, little by little."

"That's good, then." Elise thought this was the right thing to say, though her mind would not stray far from the thoughts of his lordship and her mysterious predecessors.

"Yes, it is. I'm starting to feel at home here. Are you?" Angela looked at Elise with concern.

"I suppose so. I don't know. It's strange. I don't really know what home is, in a way. It's been so long since I lived with Mummy. I suppose the school was my home, but it was still school. I like living here with you, though."

"I'm glad about that." Angela was staring into the fire now. Elise watched the light from the flames colour her cheeks. "I promised your mum, you know."

"Promised her?"

"That I'd look after you, if anything happened to her. You remember that summer she came to visit here?"

"Yes, of course." Elise's stomach squeezed in on itself tightly. It was painful to remember that happy time. Her mum had arrived in Cornwall with three days left to go of the school term. She had found a room to rent at the end of town closest to Tregynon Manor, and had seen her daughter perform in the play. She'd had tears in her eyes as she had hugged Elise afterwards. Once the school term was over, she and Elise had spent days on the beach, or walking the paths nearby. They'd had Violet with them sometimes, and on one occasion, Miss Forbes had come, too. But Annabel had only a week to spare, and that week had gone horribly fast.

"We... spent some time together then, Annabel and me. And she asked me, to make sure you were alright, if she couldn't."

Elise could feel tears shining on the surface of her eyes.

"She loved you more than anything in the world," Angela went on, unusually emotional. "You must never forget that. And now you're growing up. And you are going to attract the attention of men, and boys, and it's like a new world. I need you to know you can trust me, with anything."

Elise was caught off-guard by this short but heartfelt speech. "I do know that. Thank you," she said solemnly.

Angela smiled. "You're a good girl. Young woman, I should say, though that doesn't have the same ring to it. But you are. You stay safe and sensible."

"I'll do my best."

The very next day, the rain still drenching the town — streaming down the steep roads and bubbling along the gutters — Elise held her thin coat to her as she battled against the wind. She was going to be soaked through by the time she got to the manor.

"Need a lift?"

The car had drawn up on the other side of the road. He had opened the door and was calling to her. Lord Camelford-Bassett.

"Come on, I won't take no for an answer."

"I… well…" Not knowing what else to do, and certainly not wishing to appear rude, Elise scurried across as he opened the door for her. "Thank you," she said, shyly.

"It's my pleasure. Can't have you turning up for work all…" His eyes cast over her body. She knew her clothes were sticking to her, and felt very self-conscious. She folded her arms across her chest. She could think of nothing to say. "I see it's a bit late to save you from that," he smiled. "Not to worry. I'm sure we can find something of my wife's to fit you. Maybe something from before she had the children."

"Oh no, I, it's fine. I'll soon be dry."

"Nonsense. I'll ask Peters to fetch you something. I suppose you don't have a lot of different dresses, anyway, with the war and all. Let's see what we have at the house."

They drove in silence, the rainwater obscuring the view of the road and the sea. Elise wished she were walking.

As they travelled along the drive to the house, Elise's mind flashed back to her first view of it so many years ago, arriving as a timid schoolgirl. Who'd have imagined she'd now be working here, being driven by his lordship?

"I'll take you through the front door, save you getting any more wet. Roberts can take the car."

He was a man with whom there was no point arguing. He knew his own mind. He got his own way. He stopped the car right in front of the steps to the huge polished wooden door, and he leaned across Elise to unlatch her door. His arm brushed her legs and, as he leaned back, he let his hand brush her knee. Just for a moment; so brief, it could have been mistaken or misconstrued, but she knew he'd done it. Something stirred in her. She couldn't look at him, and felt her cheeks burning. Even so, although she knew it was wrong, for days afterwards she kept finding her mind revisiting that moment.

"Let's get you out of those wet clothes," he murmured.

Elise felt panicked inside, but she had to stay calm. This was the man she worked for, and she needed her job.

She pushed open the car door and stepped out onto the gravel, which was pooling with water in places. She walked up the steps and stood by the door. His lordship came around the side of the car and stood close to her, reaching past her to pull the bell. She marvelled at how ridiculous it was that he had to be let into his own house.

Roberts answered the door and took a look at Elise, before greeting Lord Camelford-Bassett. "A fine day, I see, sir."

"Quite right, Roberts. A perfect English spring day! I found this drowned rat on the way up here, and I've said she can have something of her ladyship's to wear. Something dry, I mean. Perhaps Peters can take her up to a guest room to dry and get changed."

Elise was relieved that at least he wasn't intending to oversee this himself. Of course he wasn't, though, she chided herself. As if he would.

"Very good, sir," Roberts rang the bell for the kitchen and Mrs Peters was soon in the large entrance hall, where she took one look at Elise and her face fell slightly.

"Mrs Peters," said the lord, "as you can see, this young lady is soaked to the skin. Would you be so good as to take her up to the Green Room and help find her some alternative clothes? We can dry these ones off for her return home at the end of the day."

"Of course, sir. Come with me, Elise," Mrs Peters said

kindly, with a note of concern.

Elise felt as though she had no choice in the matter. She was becoming used to feeling this way. Sometimes it felt like she was being carried along in life, at the will of other people, and she submitted to it without protest. When would she get to a point when she could make her own decisions?

She followed Mrs Peters, up the wide wooden stairway and around to the right.

"What happened, Elise? Why were you in the front hall?"

"I... he... his lordship was driving past, and he brought me up here in his car."

"Did he now?" Mrs Peters' mouth was a straight line. "We'll see about that. And it's his wife's clothes he's wanting you to have, is it? Well, I suppose she's enough of them. I don't suppose she'll miss anything much. Let's see if we can find something nice and plain."

Not wanting to cause any trouble, Elise let herself be shepherded into the Green Room, which had previously been a dormitory for Imogen and two of her friends. She had never been allowed in, of course, while the older girls were there, but once they had moved on and the number of girls at the house decreased, she and Violet had often found themselves in this room, reading quietly, or trying to sketch the view across the beautiful gardens. Today, that view was all but obscured, as a mist had rolled in from the sea to work with the rain. Gusts of wind had the windows rattling in their frames and raindrops threw themselves against the glass, trying to break in.

Mrs Peters was rummaging in the drawers and came back with some underwear. "Here, you can use the adjoining bathroom. Get your wet clothes off and I will hang them up for you to dry in time for this afternoon. Though it doesn't look like it's got any intention of letting up soon," she nodded towards the window. "You'll be soaked on your way home again. Unless he gives you another lift," she muttered.

"I don't want that to happen... I mean, I don't want to be any trouble. I don't mind the rain."

"You are not any trouble, my girl. Now, let's get you some warm clothes, too. Go on, into the bathroom with you."

Mrs Peters returned with some trousers, a collared blouse, and a jumper. Elise was grateful for the practical nature of the clothes, as much as for their warmth. She had started to shiver but soon felt better, although the clothes were just a little too big for her and she had to turn the trouser legs up a couple of inches. She felt nervous that the lady of the house would see her and be angry that she was wearing her things.

"Don't worry about her ladyship," Mrs Peters said, as if reading her mind. "She's away at her sister's. As usual."

It hadn't escaped Elise's notice that Mrs Peters was being even more lax than normal in her opinion of their shared employers. The woman bundled up Elise's wet things. "Come on, now, to the library with you. The children will be waiting."

"Thank you, Mrs Peters."

"It's no trouble at all. You just take care now, my girl." Mrs Peters touched Elise's cheek kindly.

"I will."

Slightly flustered and bemused, Elise walked down the main stairs to the library. Before she walked through the door, she thought she heard a low whistle and she turned, to see his lordship walking through the door to his study. He did not turn to look at her. Perhaps she had imagined the whistle.

Elise

Ever since that day when Stevie fell over, she and Maggie have waved to me every morning and every afternoon. Sometimes, I try to make myself look busy, just so they think I don't spend all day sitting looking out of my window. Sometimes, I am actually busy. Then this Wednesday just gone, they knocked at the door. Stevie presented me with a handmade card.

"I made this at school," she said proudly. "We had to think of somebody to say thank you to, and I thought of you because you looked after me when I hurt my knee."

On flimsy blue card, a crêpe paper daffodil head beamed at me, under a carefully written 'Thank you'. Inside it said,

Dear Eliz,

Thank you for helping me when I fell over.

Love Stevie xxx

"It's beautiful," I said. "Thank you so much, it's made my day. Maybe I should send you a card to say thank you for my card."

"Then I can send you one to say thanks for your card," Stevie giggled.

"That could go on for some time," I smiled.

"Actually, Elise, I was going to ask if you've got anything planned this weekend?" Maggie interjected. I sensed she was probably keen to get home. I remember those days of endless, often thankless, tasks; a never-ending 'to do' list, until it's time for bed, sleep, then waking up to yet more things to do.

I decided against making a comment about how full my diary is and opted for a straight answer. "No, nothing on this weekend... why?" I was suddenly suspicious that she might need me to volunteer for something. This is why I normally play my cards close to my chest, so that I don't suddenly find myself having to agree to helping out at a book sale to raise money for the church tower, or play group. Not very community-spirited, I know, and it's not that I'm not happy to give my time. It's more the management committees of these types of things that I try to avoid. There's always some bother over something or other, as people jostle for position. Also, if I'm honest, once you've agreed to help with one thing, it's taken as read that you have plenty of time on your hands, and would like to do every bake sale, jumble sale, craft sale going. There's one every weekend. Anyway...

"We were wondering if you'd like to come out with us? I've just got a car, you see. Nothing fancy," she quickly added. "But I'd like to take it along the coast a bit and the weather's looking promising. We thought we'd go for a walk on the beach and have some chips..."

"We don't eat fish," Stevie said proudly. "Or meat."

"Oh really? You'd get on with my granddaughter Ada, then. She's been vegetarian since she was ten."

"How old is she now?" Stevie asked.

"She's nineteen."

"Wow." Nineteen was clearly old enough to be impressive, without tipping the scales to too-old, boring adult.

"She doesn't live here, though, so I don't get to see her much." I looked at Maggie, remembering that she probably needed to get going. Fighting my natural instinct to say no, I had a quick, stern word with myself. I sit around feeling bored and lonely for much of the time, so why on earth not take up this lovely young woman's offer? "I'd love to come with you, if you're sure it's not too much trouble."

I kicked myself. I'd slipped into apologetic geriatric mode.

"Of course not. We'd love the extra company, wouldn't we, Stevie? You get a bit bored of your old mum, don't you?"

"I'm sure that can't be true," I smiled. "Anyway, I'd better let you get on your way. I'll see you on Saturday. Shall I meet you somewhere?"

"No, no, we'll pick you up. Door-to-door service," Maggie grinned, her dimples manifesting themselves. "Ten o'clock? I should warn you, we'll probably be late."

"That is absolutely fine. I'll be ready and waiting, but don't rush on my account."

On my account. I was doing it again. For goodness' sake! That was nearly a bad as *I don't want to be any bother.*

"We'll be as close to ten as possible."

"Lovely. See you then. See you, Stevie. Enjoy the rest of your week at school."

"I will!" she smiled and took her mum's hand. I stood

on the doorstep and watched their progress, Stevie skipping and chattering happily along, before they vanished round the corner and out of sight. I felt like skipping myself.

Now it's Saturday, and I've been ready since about a quarter to nine. It seems so long since I've had anything particular to get out for, where I've had to be ready for somebody else, and it was tempting to have my coat on at nine, but that would have been ridiculous. Instead, I washed my sheets and duvet cover and hung them out on the line in the garden. The sun is out today and there's a fresh wind whipping the washing, which is probably dry already. I'm looking forward to its sun-soaked scent when I climb into bed tonight.

Ten o'clock comes round and I'm in my usual window seat, bag by my side, ready to go.

Ten past ten. No sign of them. I wish I'd asked for Maggie's number, or given her mine, just in case there was a problem.

At seventeen minutes past ten, a dark blue car draws up outside, its indicator flashing on the side next to the pavement. I can see a hand waving inside, then Stevie's face presses up against the glass. I stand, and wave through my own window, hoping she can see me. Then I am up and out of the door, closing it firmly behind me and, for once, locking it. I think it's because I'm leaving the town for the day.

"Hi Elise!" Maggie is coming around the back of the car, to open the passenger door for me. "It's a bit sticky, this door, sorry." She gives it a firm pull and it opens, nearly throwing her back into me. "Oops!" she laughs and lets me in, shutting the door behind me and coming back round to the driver's side, while I greet Stevie and pull on my seatbelt.

Maggie climbs in next to me. "This is exactly the right car for us. A little bit rusty and battered, but it's in good mechanical order, apparently, and we won't be going too far, I don't suppose. It might be helpful in finding a job, though. In case I need to go a bit further afield."

"Oh, are you looking?"

"Yes, most definitely. I love volunteering, but I need to earn some money. Now Stevie's a little bit older, I feel like I can commit to something more easily." She checks her mirror, indicates, and pulls out. I hope she's a careful driver. Actually, I don't care. I'm going out for the day. She can drive as carelessly as she likes.

"What would you like to do?" I ask.

"I don't know, really. I always used to think I'd like to be a vet, or a vet nurse, but I didn't get the marks I needed in science, and I always preferred more arty subjects anyway."

"Did you have a job before you had Stevie?"

"She was a secretary," Stevie pipes up from the back. "Bor-ing."

"Hey!" Maggie says. "Not boring at all. And I wasn't a secretary as such – not that there's anything wrong with being a secretary, anyway – I was a PA. A personal assistant."

"Well, that sounds interesting."

"It was, sometimes. Sometimes it was just annoying; my boss was nice enough, but I didn't appreciate being asked to get his coffee, or his dry cleaning. I didn't get a degree to act like somebody's office wife!"

I laugh at this spirited response. "I used to work in an office," I say, turning to Stevie. "I was a secretary, in fact, at first, and you're right, it could be a bit boring. But I worked with my friend Maudie, and we did used to have a lot of fun as well."

"That's definitely a plus point of work – the people. As long as you get on with them," says Maggie. She checks the road as we reach a junction, and turns right, away from town and along one of the lanes which burrows into the farmland. It's a beautiful day, the sky at its freshest springlike blue, with thin clouds whisked across it by the ready wind.

"Yes, that's true. We worked at Fawcett's, you know, the solicitors' in town. Back in old Mr Fawcett's day."

"Oh yeah?" I can tell Maggie's mind is only half on the conversation as she concentrates on the road. I certainly had no need to worry about her driving.

"Can I go on your phone, Mum?" asks Stevie.

"OK... it's in my bag. No downloading new games though, OK? I need to save my data."

I sit back, enjoying the easy atmosphere in the car. I'm happy to just look out of the window, as the hedges and fences slip past. The roads are familiar, but it's been a long time since I've been out this way.

After twenty minutes or so, we can see the sea again, and there are a lot of white horses out there today. Maggie drives down a lane to a little car park, where sand scoots this way and that, gusting up into clouds and stinging our eyes as we exit the car.

"I'm glad I brought my coat," I remark, but my words are carried away across the dunes by a sudden gust of wind.

Maggie is helping Stevie into her coat, but Stevie shrugs away and finishes the job herself. I recognise that need for independence. It will take Maggie a little while to come to terms with the fact her daughter doesn't need her in quite the same way as she did, but she still needs her just as much as ever. I know that now.

"Sorry, Elise, I didn't realise it would be this windy!" Maggie half-shouts to me, her coat hood blowing up onto her head as though the wind is trying to protect her.

"That's quite alright," I shout back. "I really don't mind at all."

"Are you still OK for a walk on the beach?"

"Very much so." *If only you knew about my nocturnal strolls*, I think. I'm out in all weathers; except, perhaps, torrential rain, as that does tend to drench the joy out of the experience.

We walk together towards the sand, the wind whipping the breath from us, but it's exhilarating, and I think we are all laughing. It feels so good; not just the outdoors, but the refreshing, youthful company. I think of Louisa and Ada, and my stomach squeezes in slightly. I miss them physically sometimes, but I try not to let myself think too much of that.

It is near impossible to have a conversation, although I can tell Stevie is trying, holding her mum's hand and shouting into her ear. I wander happily along just behind them, letting the wind and the sea and the sand do their thing. I will be exhausted tonight, but it will be the right kind of tired. If only I'd made my bed before I left the house. Not to worry, I'll find the energy and then I can sink in between those fresh, clean sheets, and... No! Stop this. There is time for bed later, I scold myself. There is more than enough time for bed and rest and sleep almost every day.

Instead, I concentrate on the here and now. The sun and the wind waging a battle for my skin. The waves, thrashing the rocks at the end of the beach, and the gulls expertly navigating the currents of air and the frequent gusts of wind. Maggie and her daughter, holding hands and laughing at something I couldn't catch. Maggie turns to me now, asking if I know this beach.

"I do," I say, "we used to ride our bikes out here. A long time ago," I add, unnecessarily.

Maudie and I were allowed to borrow the grocer shop's bikes on a Sunday, the grocer being one of her many cousins. We'd take a picnic and a blanket and our swimming things. The beach would often be empty; there was no car park then, just a narrow path, where the road is now, and we would leave our bikes at the top, resting against a fence. Run laughingly down to the sandy shore, enjoying the one day's freedom.

Stevie pulls her mum's hand to stop and we all look down at a washed up jellyfish, iridescent and alien and smudged with grainy sand.

"That's a barrel jellyfish," I say, pulling up memories from my walks and lessons with Tabitha. "See, it's got eight frilly arms, and it's a sort of violet colour along the edge. You wouldn't want to brush up against it if you're swimming, and it might even still be able to sting you now, even though it's dead, so don't touch it. They'll avoid you in the water, though, if they can. This is a small one. They can be over a metre in diameter, when they're fully grown."

"A metre?" Stevie's eyes widen.

"Yes. Huge, isn't it?" I stretch my arms out.

It makes me want to spin, like a girl, but I can't. They'll think I'm mad. I lower my arms, and we continue on our way. We walk all the way to the end of the beach, before turning back towards the car park. When we get there, the little café is open and we go in, the walls sheltering us from the wind and meaning we can hear each other properly again.

"I'll get this," I say. "What are you having?"

"No, this is our treat," says Maggie, and I try to read the situation. I can almost certainly afford this more easily than she can, but am I going to offend her if I don't let her pay?

"I tell you what," I say, "you get the chips, and I'll get us an ice cream and a coffee after."

"OK," Maggie says. "That sounds fair."

The chips are hot and salty. I splash them with vinegar, and they are absolutely delicious.

"Nothing like some good chips after all that sea air," Maggie says.

"Mum, you always say that," Stevie rolls her eyes.

"Didn't you know, when you're a mum, you have to have regular Mum Sayings?" I put in. "You get a book of phrases, and situations where you have to use them. Does your mum always make you wash your hands before you eat?"

"Yes."

"Brush your teeth before bed?"

"Mm-hmm."

"Well, those are important things to do, and they're in that book, too. You'll see, when you have children."

"I'm not going to have children."

"Oh no? Well, I don't suppose you have to. My daughter, she didn't want children for a long time. Then she had Ada."

"I'm going to travel the world and I don't think I can do that if I have children."

"Yes, I can see how that might be more difficult. You don't have to decide now, though," I say. "Louisa, my daughter, was forty-five when she had Ada."

"That's so old!" Stevie exclaims, making Maggie and me laugh. "It is," she insists, indignantly. "Mum's not forty yet."

"I'm not far off, though, love."

"You're not going to have another baby, are you?" Stevie asks suspiciously, making us both laugh again.

"I doubt that very much," Maggie smiles and Stevie tucks into her chips once more, apparently satisfied.

We sit in the café for some time, our cheeks taking on a post-beach glow. After the chips comes ice cream, accompanied by coffee for Maggie, tea for me, and a glass of water for Stevie.

Then we have a pot of tea between us. It seems that none of us is in a hurry to leave, although at some point Stevie asks for her mum's phone again, and is drawn into some game or other while her mum and I chat, looking out across the beach and the murky, churned up sea.

I am keen to know Maggie's story, but do not want to ask her too much. Instead, it seems we talk a lot about me, and I tell her the practised version. My mum dying, my staying in Cornwall, meeting Davey, getting married, his death, our move to the house where I live now. Working at Fawcett's. Retiring. It's a fairly dull tale, but Maggie is keen to know what the town was like so many years ago. And she wants to know about Maudie, too.

"I had a friend like that," she says thoughtfully. "Back home."

Had? I think, but I don't want to pry. And I know it's painful, when you lose a best friend. Maudie was my life partner, really. Not in a sexual, or even romantic, way, but I loved her very dearly, and we'd see each other daily. Her lovely husband Fred died when we were in our late sixties and so it was just me and Maudie, for quite some time. Her loss hit me far harder than Davey's ever did.

Eventually, Maggie checks her watch. "I'm really sorry, but we're going to have to go soon. I've got a job application to fill in before tomorrow. This has been lovely, though, Elise. We'll have to do it again."

"I'd love that," I say, and I mean it. I hope she does, too, but I completely understand if she is just being polite. I feel sad that we're leaving, but when we get back to town and they insist on dropping me at my door ("I told you it was door-to-door service"), and Maggie asks if I'm free the following weekend, I feel my heart soar.

"I am," I say.

"Let's go somewhere different, shall we? Maybe you can think of somewhere, Elise. We don't know this area all that well. I bet you know all the great little beaches."

"I'll have a think," I smile. I get out of the car, trying to hide the fact I'm beginning to ache just a little bit.

"Great, well you can tell me at Caring the Community, if you're coming. Or else just knock on the window if you see us passing."

"I will," I say. "Thank you so much. I really mean it."

"It's our pleasure." She smiles as she leans across to shut the door, then indicates and pulls away. I fumble to find my key and I let myself into the house, picking the free paper up from the doormat. I get a glass of water and sit in the window seat, reading about the ongoing row between the fishing community and the company behind the Saltings development. Canyon Holdings, they're called. This argument between them and the fishermen has been going on for some time, and I can't see either side giving way.

Later, I bring my fresh sheets in, and I make my bed, getting in far earlier than I normally would, my mind full of Maggie and Stevie, who merge with Louisa and Ada as I slip into a semi-dreamlike state. I give in, and let the dreams roll in like clouds across the sea.

1948

It seemed that Lord Camelford-Bassett was around increasingly often, and no longer just on Wednesday afternoons. A hard-to-ignore presence, who might drift into the library in a 'don't mind me' kind of way, while Elise was teaching his children, or sometimes he would be out in the grounds when she was leaving for the day. It was not something she invited, or particularly wanted. Those walks to and from work were her time to herself, when she'd welcome her memories in. She was determined not to forget her home – her real home, as she still thought of it – in London, before the war, before Whiteleys, and certainly before the Camelford-Bassetts. Her few precious photos of Annabel were tucked away in her bedroom at Angela's house (despite Angela's insistence, Elise could not somehow think of it as her own home – not yet). Her recollections were still wide-ranging, but becoming more distant day by day. She wanted to remember the smell of the flat she'd shared with her mother. She wanted to remember the smell of her mother. Her voice. Sometimes, still, Annabel would appear in dreams, and then it seemed to Elise her voice came through strong and true, but if she ever tried to recreate it in her mind in waking moments, it slipped away, like a wet bar of soap.

This was her most pressing wish; to keep the memory of her mother alive. She sometimes felt it was like being adrift on the sea; an anchorless boat. All the other girls at school had talked so firmly and definitely about their homes. It never seemed to occur to them how fortunate they were.

Homes, and families, it seemed to Elise, were grounding, and provided a foundation from which to begin – and a place to return if things went wrong. Angela was kind and generous, and seemed to have thought so highly of Annabel. But she was not Annabel, and not even an aunt. Elise had no family ties. Nothing to secure her place in the world. She felt like she was cheating, and would be found out any moment.

She was grateful for the three children she taught, and how her hours with them gave her a sense of belonging. They had taken to her more or less immediately and she felt an attachment to them which she had not expected. Better than teaching in a school, she thought – she had a real insight into these children's lives.

But now there was the problem of their father. Those afternoons when he was in the garden when she left for the day; sometimes he would walk with her to the end of the drive. Never onto the road; his sense of propriety, or at least the appearance of such, prevented him from being seen in public with her, which she was grateful for. But even so, he'd take his place by her side, as if it were the most natural thing in the world. Hands behind his back, he would walk amicably alongside her. He would ask her how his children were behaving, or tell her what he and Roberts were doing to the gardens and, Elise being Elise, she would politely listen, saving a corner of her mind for Annabel. Telling her mum she would be back to her as soon as she could.

"You must miss your mother," he said one day, and he looked at her. It startled her; she had not known that he was aware of her situation, although she supposed he must be. No doubt Angela would have explained the circumstances when she first secured Elise's employment.

"I... yes, I do." She felt her mouth downturn. She'd been feeling low anyway, her time of the month approaching.

"How terrible for you. And what of your father?"

"He died, when I was a baby. I never knew him. Mummy said he was a good man."

"It's been such a time for us all. What a time to live through. My brother died, you know, in the war. And my parents both died years ago. Now it's just me."

And your wife, and your children, and your huge house, Elise thought, but she listened sympathetically. She looked at him; his grave features gazing ahead then his brown eyes flicking quickly over to her.

"I know, you must think me very self-pitying, when I have my own family. And this house."

Was she so easy to read?

"But I miss them greatly. Particularly Edmond – that was my brother's name too, you know. And my wife... well, I shouldn't speak of her, I know."

This piqued Elise's interest although, as with much about their recent exchanges, whether in words or looks, it didn't feel quite correct.

"It's just that... well, our marriage is one of... practicality, shall we say? Her parents and my parents were distant cousins, and our unity was decided long ago. As I am sure you have observed, however, it is hardly unity. She is away with her sister five days out of seven. I suspect you have seen her only a handful of times."

This much was certainly true. Having had very little experience of families, however, Elise had wondered if this was normal. The lack of time spent together. Indeed, his lordship had been largely absent during her first few weeks as well. The children spoke of 'Mother' and 'Father', as many of her schoolmates had referred to their own parents. It added an air of distance to their relationships, and felt a million miles from how things had been with her and Annabel. Sometimes when she thought back to her mum, it felt like somebody was wringing out her stomach, like it was a wet flannel. Twisting and twisting, and squeezing, hard.

How was it possible that she had lost her own mum, who wanted everything for her daughter, and wanted to be with her, but loved her so much that she would send her away? That was how Angela had explained it to Elise, more than once, until she had come to believe it. Her mum had not wanted her gone, but she had known that Elise's chances in life were greater at Whiteleys than at their local school. Plus, she was safer there, especially once the war began.

What would have happened to Elise if she'd stayed in London? She would most likely have been evacuated anyway. So many children had been. What a time to live through, as his lordship had said.

Elise walked quietly alongside him now, rolling his words around in her mind. How could she answer that? Besides, it was not a question but a statement. And she certainly did not feel equal enough to him to enter into a discussion on this topic.

"I'm sorry," he said eventually, "it was wrong of me to say that. But I do not understand my wife, and I'm damned sure she does not understand me."

These last words were spoken with a bitterness that surprised Elise. It was a relief that they had reached the end of the drive. She turned, doubtfully, to say goodbye, and he took hold of the tops of her arms. She didn't know what to do or how to react.

"Don't say a word about this to anyone, will you? I should not have said what I did."

His brown eyes on her. So earnest. Pleading, almost.

"I... of course not."

"Good girl," he smiled, making his moustache twitch, and his eyes travelled the length of her. "I know I can trust you." He flashed another smile at her, before letting her arms go.

"Goodbye, sir," she said, feeling at once a child in his presence yet somehow honoured, to be his confidant.

"I do wish you wouldn't call me sir," he said, but offered no alternative, and really, what else could she call him?

"Your lordship, then," she said, unable to help herself, and he laughed aloud, with a pleased surprise at her humour.

"Very good, Elise. Very good." And he turned back towards the house, still chuckling, leaving Elise to walk back to town, alone with her thoughts once more, but now with an unexpected spring in her step.

As the warmth of spring gradually cracked; slowly at first, as summer tentatively tapped away, like a chick inside an egg, then growing in confidence until it opened up fully, to a stern summer heatwave, the children became less willing to learn, and the library became increasingly hot and stuffy.

"Can't we have our lessons outside?" Edmond whined. "Marjorie used to let us."

"And we know what happened to Marjorie," Charles shot his younger brother a warning look.

"What did happen to Marjorie?" Tabitha asked, her eyes wide with curiosity.

"She had to go," Charles said, his tone softening as he laid a hand on his little sister's shoulder.

"But why?"

"It was something to do with... family," he said.

Elise wanted to ask him more but knew just how inappropriate that would be.

"Sometimes people have to move on," she said to Tabitha, instead, smiling around at all three children.

"You won't have to move on, will you, Elise?" The little girl's face was so open and honest, full of concern, that Elise felt suddenly like she might cry.

"Not for a long time," she said, although she knew full well that nothing was certain in this life. No promise could definitely be kept, no matter how well meant. Then, to change the subject, "Let's have lessons outside, shall we? I know the perfect place. We used to practise our plays there, when I was at school, and read our English compositions to each other."

The place she had in mind was under a huge old oak, which was at the end of a long, sweeping lawn that ran as far as the woodlands, beyond which sat the sea.

The children ran across the grass, Elise following with books and a blanket. She felt their joy at their release, and wanted to run, too. As with everywhere here, there were residual memories for her, of Violet and the rest of her friends. Lessons outside. Walks in the grounds. Scaring each other with tales of the Germans invading and creeping up through the woods. The thought made her shiver, even now.

But here she was, no longer a child. Nineteen years of

age, or near enough. She had three charges of her own, and the responsibility sat snugly on her shoulders. She spread the blanket on the grass, and called the children to her.

"We're parched!" exclaimed Edmond.

"In that case, could you run back to the house and ask Mrs Peters for a jug of cold water, and some glasses?"

"But I've only just got here!" he exclaimed.

"Well, we should have thought of it before we left the house," she acknowledged, "and we will do next time."

"You mean we can do this again?"

"Yes, if you all behave well today. If it's hot enough and nice enough, then this seems like a sensible place to learn. As long as you pay attention," she said sternly. "Charles, go with your brother to help him carry the glasses, please."

The two boys ran back across the lawn, chasing each other and holding their arms out in impressions of fighter planes.

Tabitha leant against Elise and she did nothing to discourage her. They both needed this kind of physical comfort. And she had been given such vague guidelines from the Camelford-Bassetts about what they expected of her, she was making it up as she went along. Winging it, she smiled to herself, watching the boys.

"What's all this then?" a jolly voice called from behind them, making her jump. She turned, to see his lordship approaching from the darkness of the woodlands.

"It's bright out here!" he exclaimed. "And so hot. You'd never know, under the trees."

"We thought we'd have lessons out here," Elise said, feeling like she had to justify herself. "Edmond and

Charles have just gone to get some drinks."

"I hope there's enough for me." He sat down, stretching his legs languorously, apparently unperturbed by the less than rigid nature of Elise's teaching.

Tabitha sat up straight, away from Elise.

"Hello, little one," he ruffled her hair. "Is Elise teaching you well?"

"Yes, Daddy." Not Father, Elise noticed with surprise. She had never really seen him interact with his children, or they with him. She had assumed that, with a governess and a nanny, they didn't really interact at all.

"Good. That's good. You make sure you learn like the boys, ok?"

"Yes, Daddy."

"It's too hot to learn today, though, isn't it? Should we go to the beach, do you think?"

He glanced at Elise before turning his attention back to Tabitha.

"Yes, yes!" the little girl exclaimed, her shyness receding. "Can we? Can we, Elise?"

"If that's what your father would like to do, then of course," Elise said. "Did you want me to come too, your lordship?" she asked, her eyes meeting his. That was risky, she knew, and her cheeks flushed, as she thought she really should not be so flippant with him.

"Yes, of course. We are paying you for the day, are we not, Miss Morgan?"

"You are."

"Then you must earn your wage," he fixed her eyes on her. "And today that means a trip to the beach. You will know it, I suppose? The beach belonging to Tregynon?"

"No, I... I didn't know that there was a beach here."

"I suppose not. I imagine your teachers wouldn't have wanted you girls getting into trouble down there. And it was wired off during the war anyway. It's not as sandy or as big as the town beaches, but we have it to ourselves. Don't we, little one?" He tickled Tabitha, who giggled.

"It's a steep walk down," he addressed Elise again. "Are you equal to it?"

"Yes, of course," she exclaimed, semi-indignantly. "I love walking. And I would love to see your beach."

"Good, then it's settled. Now, here come the boys. I hope they won't mind having to go back to the house again, to get their bathing things. Now, boys!" he called to them, and pushed himself up, meeting them halfway.

Edmond, after a few words with his father, which Elise could not hear, arrived at the blanket, puffing slightly. "Father says we're going to the beach!" He placed the jug of water, clinking with ice, onto the short, heat-dried grass. "Are you coming, Elise?"

"I am."

"Will you swim with us?"

"I don't think I can," she said. "My costume is at home." She was relieved; it seemed distinctly wrong to her for his lordship to see her in her bathing costume.

"Elise hasn't got a costume!" Edmond called across to his father and brother. Her cheeks flushed red-hot.

"You can borrow one," Lord Camelford-Bassett grinned, and, like so many other things, it was settled without her. She drank a glass of water, fast, and then she and Tabitha set off back to the house with the boys and her boss, to gather towels and clothes for an afternoon by the sea.

Mrs Peters raised her eyebrows at the sight of them all,

and when Tabitha told her Elise needed to borrow a bathing costume, they shot up nearly all the way to her hairline. She glanced at Elise, who looked back at her with no discernible expression.

"It was decided on my behalf," she said by way of explanation.

"I'm sure it was. Very well, let's find you something... appropriate."

Lady Camelford-Bassett had a fine collection of bathing suits, and Mrs Peters assured Elise that she was very unlikely to notice one had been used.

"I'll have it washed, dried and pressed," she said. "Now, are you sure about this? We could say it's your monthlies."

"Oh no," Elise couldn't think of anything worse than Lord Camelford-Bassett thinking about such an intimate thing. "I'll be fine. I would dearly love a swim, anyway."

"If you're sure." Mrs Peters did not look convinced.

"I am. It will make a nice change from the library."

Elise changed into the bathing suit; a deep, dark green, with a high neckline and flattering ruched waist. She slipped her dress on over the top, and gladly accepted the sun hat which Mrs Peters had also found for her.

She came into the hallway to find the three children and Lord Camelford-Bassett waiting for her. The children were excited, and she couldn't help feeling a little the same way.

They set off merrily across the lawn, Tabitha holding her hand and chattering, while Lord Camelford-Bassett chased his boys across the grass, and they laughed and shouted to each other. In the full heat of the afternoon, Elise couldn't help but smile.

The woods were dark and damp, and smelled of wild garlic. She lost her footing momentarily, Lord Camelford-Bassett catching her by the elbow to steady her.

"Thank you," she said, not wanting to look at him. She quickly moved away, addressing Tabitha, pretending she had just seen a little creature scurrying through the undergrowth.

"Where, where?" asked Edmond, the animal lover.

"I can't see it now," Elise said, "sorry, it must have scurried away."

She could just sense his lordship's smile.

The beach was in a little bay which bit sharply into the coastline. Studded with rocks, it was not as sandy as the other, bigger beaches nearby, but it had the advantage of being utterly secluded, with a gentle incline and introduction to the sea. There was a shaded spot by the rockface, which backed the beach, above which the woodland gave way. The rockface glistened in the sunshine, as tiny rivulets of water threaded their way down. The children were off, across to the seashore, immediately.

"Can you go and keep an eye on Tabitha, Elise? I'll get things set up."

Another break from the expectations set by various novels. When would the master of the house ever offer to do such menial work? Despite her better judgement, Elise found herself warming to his lordship, although she still felt shy in his presence. He was a good ten years older than her, she assumed. He must be close to thirty. And he was so self-assured; a result, she supposed, of growing up with everything he could ever need, and never being given any reason to doubt himself. The only thorn in his side she could possibly imagine was his slight limp, the origins of which were unknown, but which had saved him from going to war with the rest of his generation. Mrs Peters had informed her of this fact: "I should be grateful, really. It got us all away from here, over to the Scillies, but still I think we all felt the guilt, observing the goings-on from a distance. Not that the islands were completely removed, of course. We had a garrison there, and a fleet of planes, but the Germans decided to steer clear after a while. There were still some lives lost, my niece's husband included."

So the limp, whatever its cause, appeared to have been a blessing of sorts. And as she made her way across to the children, Elise found her mind contemplating his lordship's body; beginning with his leg, and wondering whether any injury would be visible, were he to take himself into the sea today. She should stop right there, she knew, and was glad that she was between him and the children, alone with her thoughts for just a moment, as if any of them could tell what she'd been thinking about, before she composed herself.

"Elise! Elise! Watch this!"

Before she had a chance to stop him, Edmond had crashed, fully clothed, into the sparkling sea.

"Wait…" she called uselessly, and glanced back to see what reaction this foolhardiness would bring from his father. But his lordship was laughing, and pulling off his shoes. Elise quickly turned her attention back to the children.

"Edmond!" she admonished, when the boy's head, slick and wet like a seal's, appeared above the surface. At least he'd had the sense to take his shoes and socks off. He came back onto the shore, his clothes clinging to his little frame.

"Take them off, Edmond, and put them on that rock over there, to dry," Elise instructed, thinking how the clothes would be crisp with salt when they dried.

Meanwhile, his brother had stripped unashamedly down to his shorts, and their little sister was standing close to the shallows, watching the goings on with apparently little compulsion to join them. As Charles made his way in, more tentatively than Edmond, Elise heard the sound of footsteps running up behind her, then she was overtaken by the children's father, who had also undressed as far as his shorts and was now dashing headlong into the gentle waves, splashing his sons and laughing out loud. Elise moved her full attention to Tabitha, who was trying to undo the buckles on her shoes.

"Here, let me help you," Elise said, and the little girl put her hands on Elise's head to steady herself. Her small, soft feet revealed, she looked at Elise.

"Your turn now."

"Oh, I..." The sun-soaked water was too much to resist, with the slightest breeze playing across the tops of the waves, and the light bouncing off.

"Go on, then." Elise took off her own shoes, and contemplated her bathing costume. Did she dare take her dress off? Was it hugely improper, with just the children and their father, and herself?

Just do it, she heard a voice inside her head. Was it Angela's? Annabel's? Her own? *Why should you stand baking in this heat while everyone else is having so much fun? Besides*, it continued more sneakily, *Tabitha won't go in without you.*

Taking her hat off, she waited a moment, until she could see that his lordship was engaged in a battle with his sons, then she shyly pulled her dress over her head and folded it quickly, placing it on top of her shoes. Then she picked up Tabitha, partly as a way of obscuring her body in the bathing costume, and carried her into the water, the little girl's arms around her neck, and legs around her waist. Elise couldn't look at the others, but bobbed down so that her body and Tabitha's were immersed in the cold saltwater. The girl shrieked and clung on tighter. Elise risked a glance at his lordship and saw he was smiling across at her. She offered a small smile in return, then turned her back on him, shielding the little girl from the waves, such as they were.

With the sun on her shoulders and the back of her neck, Elise longed to swim freely; to give herself over to the sea, for a while at least. But soon Tabitha had had enough and wanted to go back in to shore. Elise stood to her full height, accepting this was her role, but she heard his voice behind her. "I'll take her, Elise. If you'd like a swim. You would like a swim, wouldn't you?"

Lord Camelford-Bassett was just metres away; bare-chested and glistening.

"I... well, I..." *Do it*, came that voice. *Take the opportunity.* "That would be lovely. If you're sure."

"I'm sure," he said, approaching with his arms open to his daughter. Tabitha turned and held one arm out towards him, the other still holding on to Elise. In the transfer of the warm little body, Elise felt the skin of her arm and his lordship's cross paths; the water creating a kind of friction between them. His arms were hairy, as was his chest, she realised, and she felt her cheeks redden at the contact. He seemed not to notice, however, taking his daughter confidently and swinging her around so that she giggled with pure glee. It was only as he turned to walk away that he threw a glance and a smile Elise's way. She plunged headlong into the safety of the water, feeling the bubbles pushing up around her until she emerged again, eyes stinging with salt and blinking in the sunlight.

The two boys were farther out, Elise saw, both practising their swimming, and egging each other on. She swam out to them, using the strong, confident front crawl she had learned while at school.

"You're a good swimmer," Charles said admiringly.

"Well, thank you."

"Can you teach me to swim like that?"

"I can try," she said.

"Me too!" Edmond exclaimed, never one to be left out.

For the next thirty minutes or so, the three of them swam back and forth across the mouth of the little inlet, Elise instructing and demonstrating and the boys catching on quickly. She was reluctant to leave the water, but after a time they were all tired and thirsty.

"Shall we go in now, Elise? Before we get cramp?"

"Yes, alright. I suppose we should."

She followed the boys to the shallows and onto the sand, where they each collected their belongings, Edmond retrieving his clothes from the rock.

"They're dry already, Elise!" he said.

"That's good," she smiled. "Just make sure you get them to Mrs Peters when you've changed back at the house."

Now what should she do? Put her dress straight back on over her wet costume? She could not walk boldly up the beach without it on, she decided, so she pulled the dress over her head, instantly aware of the way it was clinging to her body. There was no modest option in this situation, but this still seemed the preferable one.

As they walked up the beach, the rough sand pleasingly scratchy under her feet, she looked up to see Tabitha running to meet her. She scooped her up, the girl a shield once more, and approached the blanket.

"Lemonade, Elise?" Lord Camelford-Bassett asked.

She had not had lemonade since the day the war ended, when somebody had somehow found a crate of glass bottles and issued small paper cups to everyone round and about.

"Yes, please." The thought of the sharp, sweet drink quenching the salty taste of her mouth. "That would be lovely."

"You'd better put Tabitha down, then." He smiled, proffering a cup.

Elise did as she was told, aware of herself once more, but he simply smiled and handed her the cup, then poured one for each of the boys.

In the heat of the afternoon, Elise soon dried off, her hair still tightly pinned up and just the odd strand escaping. The children were content to play nearby and for a while it was just her and Lord Camelford-Bassett, seated at either side of the blanket.

"Tell me about your war, Elise," he said.

"My war?"

"Yes. How was it, for you? In the school? And losing your mother. If you don't mind me asking, that is."

"I don't mind," she said, looking him in the eye, and finding that she meant it. Nobody had really asked her before. "It was… in a way, it was the same as ever, being at school. Just in a different place. A beautiful place," she said with feeling. "The sea… I'd never seen the sea before we came here. Now I don't think I ever want to leave it."

"I know what you mean. Exactly what you mean." His eyes were on the vast expanse before them. A sailing boat was crossing their view, far out. "And your mother. Do you mind me asking?"

"No. She… she was wonderful. She was a nurse. She got hit by a bomb, like thousands of people did. I don't really like to think about it."

"No. I don't suppose you do. My parents both died when I was young. I told you that, didn't I? So we have that in common, Elise. Both orphans at a young age."

She didn't know what to say. They certainly did not have much more in common. He had been left with a huge estate. She had been left with nothing but her brain and the kindness of strangers.

"I miss my mother, but I don't miss Father," he said. "He was a bastard."

Elise was shocked at his language, and remained quiet.

"I'm sorry to speak in such a way, but it's true. You must think it awful of me to speak like that about my dead parent. But I feel no sense of loss about him."

"I don't think it's awful. People are different. Not everybody is worth missing."

"No!" he laughed. "Exactly that. Not everybody is worth missing." He looked at his watch. "Speaking of missing, we'd better get ourselves back to the house. My wife is due back late this afternoon and if we are not there when she arrives, it will not go down well."

Elise found herself disappointed, at the abrupt end to the afternoon at the beach, and even more, she realised, at the thought of her ladyship's return. But of course, she must come back to her home, and her family.

"I'll tell the children," she said. "Then I'll gather our things together."

"We can both do that," he smiled, and they walked across to the rocks, where the three children were poking about in the warm, shallow pools. Disappointment was written across their faces when they were told that their fun was over.

"Can we do it again, Father?" Charles asked.

"With Elise?" pleaded Edmond. "She's teaching us how to front-crawl."

"I saw," Lord Camelford-Bassett smiled. "She's a very good swimmer. I'm sure that you boys can come down with her, anyway."

"Thank you, Father!" Charles exclaimed but Elise couldn't help but feel slightly disappointed again, at the thought it might just be her and the boys next time.

At Tregynon Manor, his lordship went to his rooms and the children to theirs, to change, while Elise went to the kitchen, where preparations for dinner were underway.

"I'll get going," she said to Mrs Peters.

"Good afternoon, was it?" The older woman smiled.

"Yes, it was lovely. The boys are such good swimmers."

"They're very fond of you."

"And I of them."

"I know. I hope you'll stay."

"I have every intention of it."

"Then good, I'm glad. Now, get yourself back to the Green Room and changed again, before her ladyship returns."

Not waiting to be told twice, Elise turned on her heel. Was she imagining it, or was there was something not very comfortable about the prospect of Lady Camelford-Bassett coming back? Nobody seemed overly enthused at the idea; but was that just wishful thinking, and also inappropriate? She was, after all, just a servant to this family, and entirely disposable.

She changed her clothes and brought the bathing costume down to the kitchen, as Mrs Peters had assured her she would wash it and have it back in the closet where it belonged. Dinner smelled delicious and Elise realised she was famished after the afternoon at the beach.

"You've caught the sun, my dear. It suits you," Mrs Peters said approvingly. "Now go on, off to your home and your tea. I'll see you tomorrow."

"You will. Thank you, Mrs Peters."

"My pleasure."

As she set off walking down the drive, Elise heard the sound of a car. She stood aside to let it past. Mr Roberts, who was driving, smiled at her, and Elise caught a glimpse of Lady Camelford-Bassett, whose eyes met hers coolly. Elise went to raise her hand in greeting but the woman had already turned away.

She was a strange match for his lordship, whose easy, friendly nature was so at odds with his wife's. But that hadn't been apparent at first, she reminded herself, thinking how aloof and abrupt he had once seemed. Maybe her ladyship was the same. And, Elise reminded herself, it was not her place to make judgements about her employers.

She set off walking again, glad that it was Angela's turn to cook tonight. She would have a piece of bread when she got in, though, with some butter if they had any.

Her mouth watering and her thoughts now turned to food, she nearly missed him.

"Elise," he said, emerging from the trees near the end of the drive. "I'm glad I caught you. I wanted to thank you for being such a sport this afternoon."

"That's quite alright," she said politely. "It was the perfect thing to do on such a hot afternoon."

"I enjoyed it," he said, moving towards her. "The children did, too. I hope that we can do it again."

He was standing quite close to her now; too close to be entirely proper, she thought, as she looked up into his face. A wild thought came to her, that he was going to kiss her. But he smiled, and brushed the back of his hand softly across her cheek instead.

"Dinner," he said, and she wondered for a moment if she'd heard him correctly.

"Dinner," she agreed, and she stepped away slightly. But as Elise walked back to town, all thoughts of dinner were banished from her mind.

Elise

The outings with Stevie and Maggie have become quite regular; if not every week, then every other week. I am pleased, but I can't help feeling slightly uncomfortable about it. Am I a charitable cause? I can't believe they actually want to spend time with an old duffer like me. But I also do not wish to be ungrateful, and I am delighted at the prospect of getting out of town again. Much as I love it here, I can't deny it's good to have a change of scenery, and not see the same old faces, or have the same old conversations.

Today, we're going to Lanhydrock – a National Trust place. Stevie is going on about hiring bikes and I can tell Maggie is thinking, *We can't very well do that with Elise, can we?*

"Why don't you two hire bikes while I have a look around the house?" I suggest. "It's been a long time since I've visited Lanhydrock, and I'd like to acquaint myself with it again. I may be wrong, Stevie, but I'm thinking you might not have a lot of interest in the house?"

"Erm..." she says, her eyes darting to her mum.

"It's fine!" I laugh. "Maybe I'm doing you a disservice, but I bet you'd rather get out and about in the woods than look around a stuffy old house."

My turn to cast my eyes towards Maggie now. I hope I'm saying the right thing. What if she hates bikes, and wants to look around the house, too?

She is smiling, though. "I think that sounds like an excellent idea, Elise, if you're sure you don't mind. I could do with burning off a bit of energy – and a few pounds!"

"I hardly think that's true, my love," I say, and I mean it. She's not a skinny Minnie, that's for sure, but she's a beauty, is Maggie. One of those women who has no idea of it, though. And she doesn't dress it up. I don't think I've seen her wear anything other than jeans, or those army-style trousers, like she's got on today. I can't imagine ever wearing anything like that, but we're of such different generations. I do favour trousers, but I like light, chino-style, which still look neat and trim, and allow much more activity than skirts.

My mum, and Angela, were always trouser-wearers. High-waisted and wide-legged, in Mum's case (unless she was working, when she had to wear the standard issue nurse's uniform: "Dresses are so impractical," she used to complain, but she did look smart in it), and calf-length pedal-pushers for Angela. I have a picture of them both together, from that summer Mum came to Cornwall. They're standing by the railings on the harbour, smiling in the sun. Mum is pushing a strand of her long red hair from her eyes.

It's the last image I have of her, save my memories of saying goodbye at the train station, when she had to leave. That memory still provokes such sadness in me now.

I must have sighed as Maggie sends a slightly curious glance my way, but she doesn't ask anything. I like that about her. She is interested without being nosy.

When we get to Lanhydrock, we go our separate ways. The place has changed, and yet somehow remains the same. It is visitor-friendly in that pleasant, modern way now, with wide, even paths suitable for wheelchairs, pushchairs, and toddlers on those little pedal-free bikes they have these days. When I last came here, in the late 1940s, it still belonged to the family who eventually bequeathed it to the National Trust. They were acquaintances of Lord and Lady Camelford-Bassett, who I was working for at the time.

Today, I take my place in a slow-moving train of visitors, consulting guidebooks and maps, and listening to the knowledgeable tour guides. I know a different side to this place, I think. But who would believe me? Who would listen? I'm just another aged visitor, here to see how the other half lived so many years ago.

I learn more today about the family who lived here back then, and how it was the First World War which changed the face of the place. While the boys went off to the Front, the women of the family took on roles in the war effort; working in a way which never would have been thought of if the men were still at home. One of the daughters, Constance, became a nurse, and remained in this profession even after the war. It makes me think of Mum, as so many things do. She and Constance so different, in their upbringings, and material status, but both drawn to the same profession.

I shuffle along obediently, and try not to show any reaction when we reach the rooms where his lordship and her ladyship stayed. I had my own room, of course, up in the attic with the other servants.

It's a strange feeling, looking at the place from behind

a thick rope. I feel detached from it. An outsider now, as I suppose I was then, really. I still feel relief when I exit into the grounds and go to find Maggie and Stevie.

They are waiting for me by the adventure playground, where it appears Stevie has found some friends. Two boys who I am assuming are brothers. Maybe even twins.

"From school," Maggie says. "I told her she could play with them while we sit out here and have our sandwiches. I hope you don't mind."

"Of course I don't," I smile, and look across to Stevie, who is climbing steadily and confidently up a roped climbing frame, the two boys flanking her on either side.

"I like her having company her own age," Maggie says. "As she's an only child."

"I can understand that. I was an only child, too. It was just me and Mum, like you and Stevie. But then there were the girls at school. I wouldn't say they were like sisters as such, but we were a family. A large, and slightly strange, family."

Maggie laughs. "I did want more children," she tells me.

"Oh yes? Well, you're still young."

"I guess… but I'm getting older. And I need a man if I want a baby!" She blushes at her own choice of words. "I suppose the problem is, I'm not sure I want another one of those."

"There are other ways," I say. "These days, there are women doing it themselves. Not, you know…" my turn to blush. I'm too old to blush.

"I know what you mean," Maggie quickly responds with her ready smile. "Sperm donors. Adoption. I don't know. It's an expensive business, just keeping a child alive and clothed, never mind shelling out to have another one!"

"True enough. And you don't have a boyfriend now?"

"No, I… let's just say the last one was enough trouble to put me off. Better to keep it just me and the girl. What happened to your husband?" she ventures.

"He died."

"Oh, I'm sorry. That must have been hard."

"Not especially," I say, judging that I can say this to Maggie, and she might 'get it', as Louisa used to say ("You just don't get it, Mum." I get a lot more than you might think).

Maggie gives me an assessing look. "Was he… were you not happy?"

"No, I was very unhappy with Davey."

"I'm sorry," she says again.

"Yes, well, it was the way of things. I don't mean to sound callous about him. I hadn't wanted him to die, but I had wanted him out of my life."

"I think that's understandable. I… can I talk to you, Elise?" Maggie's big brown eyes are on mine. Searching for something. It's trust, I think. Maybe it's a safe place she needs.

"Of course you can. I'm good at keeping secrets."

"Well, it wasn't exactly a straightforward relationship. There was a lot of hurt. It was over before it had begun, really, but then there I was pregnant, and he was nowhere to be seen."

"That's terrible," I say, so pleased that she feels able to talk to me.

"Yes, well, I don't suppose I behaved perfectly, either. But anyway, he's the reason we're here, me and Stevie. He'd moved away, you see, but now he's back."

"But you shouldn't have had to move. That's completely wrong. Though I'm glad for my sake that you did!"

Over her shoulder, I can see Stevie laughing with the boys, as they run across the soft wood-chipped floor. They're so young, I think. On equal footing. I hope that they keep that as they grow up.

"It's fine. Well, it's not. But we're happy, Stevie and I. Maybe happier than we were before, I think. She didn't really like her old school but she loves where she is now."

"And what about your family? I bet they miss you."

"We kind of… fell out," she says, sadly. "My dad died, a year or two ago, and it upset the balance somehow. My sister and I – we're twins, you know – used to get on really well. Not always, of course, but we had the same friends when we were growing up, and we really were very close. But she always got on with my mum, better than I did – and I got on with Dad. When he died, everything changed. Mum was heartbroken, and began to spend a lot more time with my sister and her boys. She's got three sons, and Mum worships them. Sorry, I'm going on a bit here."

"Not at all," I put my hand on hers. "It sounds like you need to get it out."

"You're very kind, Elise. Thank you. I suppose our family changed when Dad died, and we haven't been able to recover what we had."

"That's sad."

"Yes. It is. I did have a lovely childhood. And I do love my mum, and my sister. But she's cross with me because of what happened, with Stevie's dad."

"Well, that's not fair!" I feel outraged on my new friend's behalf.

"Maybe, maybe not," she says.

There's something more to this, I think, but I don't want to pry. No doubt it will all come out in its own good time. But there is a sadness there, in Maggie, that I feel I can identify with, though it may come from a different source to my own.

Eating sandwiches seems incongruous with the conversation we're having but nevertheless, we take regular bites, the soft, springy bread and sharp mature cheddar all the more satisfying for being in the fresh air. Maggie turns to watch her daughter and for a while we don't speak much more.

1949

When the invitation to Lanhydrock came, Elise heard the Camelford-Bassetts talking in the hallway. Their presence had been requested for a weekend at the beautiful stately home. She was sitting in the library, waiting for the children. The open doorway allowed her to hear the whole conversation.

"I do not have a maid," Lady Camelford-Bassett complained. "How can I hold my head up, when the other ladies will have their maids with them?"

"Patricia Wilding does not have a maid," his lordship said.

"I am not Patricia Wilding," his wife replied. "No, I cannot go unless I have someone to see to my needs."

"Then we cannot go, and it's no great loss to me," he said.

"But we must go!"

"I can't win," he sighed dramatically, and Elise suppressed a smile. She could not say that she had warmed to her ladyship, who barely even gave her the time of day. Suddenly, Lord Camelford-Bassett was at the door. She sat up straight. "Elise, are you busy in three weekends' time?"

"I don't believe so. No more than normal." There were dances at weekends, which she often resolved to attend, but it was hard without Violet by her side, and so far she had not summoned up the courage.

"Could you see your way to coming to a weekend party, at Lanhydrock Manor? To help my wife with her... things."

"I... I suppose I could..."

"I know you are not a lady's maid, and I would like you to understand I do not see you as such. You are our children's governess. But Lanhydrock is a beautiful house, and they are good people. You will be well looked after, and we shall pay you for your troubles, of course. It will just be a matter of looking after her ladyship's clothing, hair, and so on. Could you do that, do you think?"

Elise could not think of anything she would dislike more. "Yes, of course, if you need me."

"I think it is a case of want rather than need, but I appreciate your willingness. There, my dear," he called to his wife, who appeared in the doorway. "It is settled. Elise will pretend to be your maid, and all will be well."

Lady Camelford-Bassett had the decency to look slightly abashed, although Elise could see she was also quite pleased at the thought. "Thank you, Elise." It was the first time she had said her name – and in fact the first time she had said thank you.

"You're welcome, your ladyship."

"Now, I must plan my wardrobe. Perhaps you could help?" Lady Camelford-Bassett said, almost eagerly.

"The children must learn," his lordship said sharply. "It is enough that we are dragging Elise away from her home for a weekend. We cannot also drag her away from her work, with our children. You will have to make these all-important wardrobe decisions yourself."

Colouring slightly, Lady Camelford-Bassett turned and left. Elise felt embarrassed, perhaps even a twinge of sympathy, at hearing his lordship talk to his wife that way.

"Thank you, Elise," he said again, once his wife was out

of earshot. "I appreciate this. And it will be good for me to have your company."

Elise looked up sharply, but they were disturbed by the sound of the children chattering as they came down the stairs. Elise pulled her shoulders back and stood up, ready to greet her charges. His lordship smiled, turned, and followed his wife's footsteps.

"They want you to do what?" Angela had exclaimed indignantly, when Elise told her what she had been asked to do. "Good god, you're an educated young woman. And she has surely learned to dress herself and do her own hair?"

"I think it's because the other ladies have them."

"*Ladies*," Angela tutted indignantly, her brow darkening at the word. "That's half the problem right there. Women expecting to be 'ladies'. Men expecting us to be 'ladylike'. We are girls, then we are women. No amount of money or breeding makes any one of us any better than another."

"I know. And you are right. It is all a bit meaningless, and I know it's all about appearances. I know that I am no less than my employers." And she did know this, but then faced with the Camelford-Bassetts and their way of speaking... way of being... she found herself floundering a little. Wondering if she was, in fact, below their station. "But Lord Camelford-Bassett said Lanhydrock is a fine house, and the people are nice, and I'll be well looked after."

"He did, did he?" Angela had huffed slightly. "Not as well looked after as they'll be, I'm sure. It'll be them upstairs and you downstairs, when you're not combing her ladyship's hair, that is. For goodness' sake, a grown woman expecting somebody else to comb her hair for her." Angela tugged at her own hair, which she wore in a short, neat bob. "Think you can do anything with this?" she said, recovering her sense of humour.

"I'll see if I can pick up any tips."

They had reached an easy kind of friendship now, Elise and Angela. The teacher-pupil status was a thing of the past, and Elise was glad. She was also grateful that Angela did not try to be a stand-in for her mother. Instead, she treated Elise with respect, and almost as an equal. Age was the thing which stood the two of them apart – that and experience.

"And watch out for these so-called 'gentlemen', you hear me? Some of them have a very liberal interpretation of the word."

Elise had flushed, Lord Camelford-Bassett springing straight to her mind. Angela took the colour in her face to be embarrassment caused by youthful naivety. Elise had let her previous suspicions dwindle away, never mentioning again the attention that he paid to her. It was silly, she knew, but she felt like she needed to protect him. In some way he had shown a vulnerability to her, and she didn't like Angela casting aspersions on him.

"I mean it. You're a pretty young woman. You wouldn't be the first lady's maid to be made a pass at by a lord, or an earl, or a duke, or whatever. What?" she exclaimed, seeing Elise was about to protest. "You might as well know. Then you'll be prepared."

"I was about to say I'm not a lady's maid," said Elise.

"That's really not the important part."

Elise travelled separately to the Camelford-Bassetts, there being far too little room in one car for a driver, the married couple, and all of her ladyship's bags. Elise instead was transported with the luggage on the first car journey, and ushered into the beautiful grand house and up to the allocated rooms, where she could begin unpacking, while Mr Roberts returned to make the second journey.

It was very strange being in this huge house, in the beautifully furnished bedroom. There was a hush about the place, although on the way from the servants' staircase along the spotless, polished corridor, she had heard activity behind closed doors; presumably other guests, or their servants, unpacking and preparing for the weekend. The gentlemen were set for a day's shooting on the Saturday, while the ladies would be out riding. What Elise was meant to do during this time, she had no idea. Presumably just be there for her ladyship's every whim. It was a role which did not sit comfortably with her, and she would have liked to have been able to explore the house and grounds at her leisure. She also could well imagine her mum's reaction, had she known her daughter would be acting as a lady's maid. *I didn't send you to that school so you could spend your life waiting on somebody else.*

It was just temporary, though, Elise reminded herself. Her real job was a governess. Teaching. Though that could not last forever, it would give her a chance to think about what it was she really wanted to do with her life. And maybe soon she could build up her social life. Make some local friends. Between the children and Angela, all of whom she loved, she was feeling the need for some company of her own age.

When the Camelford-Bassetts arrived, Elise was flustered, at the thought of being in a room with a married couple – and particularly, if she was honest, his lordship. It was silly, she knew, and was embarrassed that she even felt that way, but if she couldn't be honest with herself then what was the point?

As it turned out, however, she didn't even see him. He had his own room, which he went straight to, while her ladyship bustled into her own quarters, all ready for Elise to pamper her. The two rooms were adjoined by a private bathroom, on either side of which were highly polished, ornate wooden doors, leading into the bedrooms.

"They'd use that when they visited their mistresses," Lady Camelford-Bassett said while she sat having her hair brushed, a little later. "Back when that kind of thing went on. These days it's different, you know." Elise thought she didn't look too sure. She said nothing, and carried on brushing out her ladyship's long blonde hair; so fine and smooth, and different to her own.

At dinnertime, the servants ate downstairs in the servants' hall, whilst the brother and sisters who lived at this vast place, and their invited guests, dined in the grand dining hall on the ground floor. Elise felt shy making her way down, but had of course met a couple of the house staff already and found everybody welcoming. It was quite an eye-opener, in fact, and she sat quietly, while the others, who all seemed well-acquainted, talked and laughed loudly, often at the expense of their employers.

Elise smiled politely and kept her counsel. She must

have been a good couple of years younger than the youngest of the others. There were three other lady's maids, who seemed to know each other well already, and sat in a tight little knot at the other end of the table. They weren't unfriendly, but it seemed they had much to say and catch up on. Meanwhile, Elise was seated with the Lanhydrock staff, of which there were many more than at Tregynon, where it really was just her, Geraldine the nanny, Mr Roberts and Mrs Peters.

Georgie, who had shown her to her room, seemed to be the friendliest, and she included Elise in the conversations as much as possible, but it always seemed there was somebody else ready to speak, more loudly and more urgently, and in the end Elise just sat back and enjoyed the food and the atmosphere, smiling and laughing when she thought it appropriate. Her head was starting to ache, and she was looking forward to going to bed.

Before that, however, she must help her ladyship be ready for her own bed. Elise was notified of this by the head of the staff at Lanhydrock. Apparently, Lady Camelford-Bassett was feeling tired. Elise found she was grateful for the excuse to leave.

Would Lord Camelford-Bassett be visiting his wife in her room tonight, Elise wondered as she made her way up the back staircase. She was awed by the scale of the place, and worried she would get lost, but she found the room alright, only shortly before her ladyship arrived.

"The men are sitting up, there's talk of cards. I don't feel like it," Lady Camelford-Bassett said, as she took her place at the dressing table. Elise thought she seemed a bit defensive.

"So I've come to bed, ready for the riding tomorrow," her ladyship continued breezily. "If you can brush and plait my hair and help me with my nightclothes."

Help her with her nightclothes? Annabel's scornful voice came to Elise once more. *Has she lost the use of her arms? Honestly, Elise, get out of there. This is not for you.*

It's just temporary. A one-off, Elise reassured herself.

She did as she was bid. Lady-Camelford-Bassett looked younger, with her hair tied back. Her ears stuck out a little, Elise realised, which for some reason endeared the woman to her more. Once she was in her nightdress, her ladyship told Elise that she could go.

Thank god for that, the girl thought, exhausted. It was the pressure of this strange situation, and not being able to relax, even at dinner. She made her way to the servants' corridor, hearing laughter – men's and women's – from downstairs. So, it wasn't just the men who were staying up late. Maybe Lady Camelford-Bassett wasn't as comfortable in this setting as she'd like to be.

In the dimly-lit corridor, Elise thought she would like some fresh air before bed. She took the stairs down, hoping she could slip outside unnoticed. She was grateful that she didn't see anybody else, but could hear laughter coming from the direction of the servants' hall as well. She was glad to leave it behind her, and could not wait to be back home with Angela.

Home. It was the first time she had thought of it as such. Sunday night, in front of the fire. Nothing to do but put her feet up, and drink a nice cup of tea, and make sure she was never in this position, ever again.

Still, while she was here, she might as well make the

most of it, and to her it was the thought of the beautifully tended grounds that was most enticing.

She slid her way through the shadows, in between the trees of the formal garden. The moon was high, sending pools of light across the manicured lawns, and she kept close to the edges, out of sight from the house.

"Elise," came a surprised, but pleased, voice. "What are you doing out here?"

She jumped at the sound of her name, her heart beating fast in her chest. Turning, she saw his lordship, who was looking at her, amused.

"Are you meant to be out here?" he asked.

"Her ladyship's in bed, sir, I just wanted some fresh air."

"I'm just teasing, I'm sorry. I'm glad you have the chance to get out. I'm sorry about... you shouldn't be doing this... Alicia doesn't need..." his voice drifted off.

"It's alright. She's nice to me."

"That's not really the point," he said, through gritted teeth. "It's all for show, isn't it? All of this," he gestured to the house, with his glass. "Tregynon. It's not real. It's not how real people live. Not how you live, is it, Elise?"

Lord Camelford-Bassett stood full in the moonlight. He was not afraid of being seen. The liquid in his glass sloshed dangerously.

"Aren't we all real? None of us more or less than others." Where had that come from? And should she really be talking to her employer like this?

"You're right," he laughed. "None of us more or less. Well said, Elise, well said." He moved closer, sharing the shadows with her. "You're a clever young woman, aren't you?"

"I…" This felt uncomfortable. Distinctly wrong. But she didn't move away. She didn't dare. And if she was very, very honest, she didn't quite want to.

"You can say it, you know. No need to be embarrassed by it, or try to hide it. God, I hope Tabitha grows up proud of who she is. I hope she has a brain."

"She does, I am sure of it."

"You must help her use it. So she doesn't want to be a *lady* with a maid, and a trunk full of dresses, and a head full of hot air."

Elise's face burned at the thought of this disloyalty to his wife, but also with a little pride, that he thought she was different. He thought she was clever. And he didn't seem to like his wife much. But he seemed to like her.

His breath smelled strongly, of what she presumed must be whisky, or brandy perhaps. She took a step back.

"I should be going."

"You don't have to go anywhere you don't want to." He put his hand on her arm and looked into her eyes.

If only you knew, she thought. He was older than her. Educated. He'd seen the world. But did he really think she was able to make the kind of choices he could? She needed her job, and she needed Angela's generosity. She was far from free and, yes, she did have to go places she didn't want to. She had to do things she didn't want to do, too.

But those eyes. And his proximity to her. They were hard to ignore, and she found she couldn't look away. She tried to step back, but his fingers tightened slightly on her.

"Don't go, not yet. Don't make me go back to those bores."

Elise was not particularly shockable. She'd been through enough to know what a real shock was. It was losing your mum to a bomb. Nevertheless, she was a little shocked at just how irreverent this conversation was becoming. But she imagined it probably was a bit boring in there. These people must just mix with their own kind, all the time. And there were not all that many of their own kind to keep things interesting. And then, what if you didn't like them? The other lords and ladies? It would be like being stuck at Whiteleys with Imogen rather than Violet.

"I... don't think I can save you from that, sir."

"Enough of the 'sir'!" he exclaimed. "Honestly, enough of it all." He looked away, took his hand off her arm. Elise allowed herself a slow exhale, but before she had the chance to even half-empty her lungs, he was before her, his hands gently cupping her face and his lips on hers.

A kiss. She had never been kissed before; never like this, and not in any way for years. Not since Annabel had visited. And she could not remember ever being kissed by a man. Not her own father, an uncle, or a grandfather. It was just her, and her mum, and that was the way it had always been.

Do not underestimate the power of the human touch, especially when it has been absent for such a long time. Elise felt his strength and his solidity, firm and definite, his height reduced as he stooped slightly to bring his face to hers. The warmth of his lips, and the infinitely strange bristle of his moustache. And an awakening in her, of something undefined but present in her these last few years, just out of reach.

She let him kiss her. She would scarcely have known

how to say no anyway, but the truth is she did not want to. In years to come, she would look back and think how wrong it all was, but in that highly-charged moment it felt right.

His arms went around her, pulling her in to him. She felt small, yet somehow powerful. He wanted her. Not his wife, but her. He groaned slightly and it disturbed something within her. Something almost maternal – but not quite.

And then... laughter. Not his. But definitely male.

Two voices, close by, causing Lord Camelford-Bassett to release her so fast that she almost fell to the floor.

"Taking full advantage of the wife's early night, eh, Andrew?"

Elise realised she hadn't even known his first name until now.

"Go to hell," his lordship said, then, "Go to your room, Elise."

Go to your room. From sexual desire to being treated like a child, in one fell swoop. Elise turned and fled, her cheeks red, and her eyes full of angry tears. She found her way to the servants' corridor and up the back stairs, not caring whether or not she passed anybody on her way. Up to her room she ran, and there she sat on the hard single bed, her head in her hands and full of angry thoughts, but not towards him. Simply towards herself. What a fool she was.

In time, there was a knock on the door. It was Georgie.

"Madam says you're needed back home," she said knowingly, but not unsympathetically. "Brockhurst will drive you. Gather your things and follow me."

Elise did as she was bid, and followed the young woman

back down the stairs, through the now-empty servants' hall, and out into the night. The moon was still bright above as she climbed into the car.

"Back to the town is it, miss?"

"Yes, please."

"Just you let me know your address, and I'll get you there."

"Thank you." His kindness was enough to bring fresh tears to her eyes. She sat back and let them come, as the car bumped along the winding drive and into the open arms of Cornwall. Shame and relief mingled with her tears, knowing that she should not have let that happen, and wondering who had ordered her removal. His lordship, her ladyship, or one of the Lanhydrock family? Were they all talking about her now? She imagined she would be the main topic of conversation at one of the breakfast tables tomorrow, if not both – downstairs, for sure.

"I hope your aunt will be alright," she heard the driver's voice.

"My aunt?"

"Yes, did Georgie not say?" he asked, despairingly. "Honestly, that girl. Lord Camelford-Bassett had word that your aunt is poorly. A telephone call from one of his staff. I'm sorry, I thought you knew. He said you would want to be with her. And you're not to bother coming to work on Monday. He's a good man, that one."

"He... he is," she said weakly, almost questioningly, wondering how on earth he had managed this, and angry at herself for how pathetically grateful she was towards him. How would it be, when she saw him back at Tregynon, she wondered.

Then it hit her. *You're not to bother coming to work on Monday.* That was it, then. Just like that, she had lost her employment. He had got her – and himself – out of a sticky situation, but it was clear he did not want to see her again. Why had he kissed her, if she meant so little to him? More importantly, what was she going to tell Angela?

Elise

It's a fresh Saturday morning, and the clocks are turning forward tonight. I've risen with the sun, too excited to sleep any longer. Today, Louisa is coming.

I'm up and out early, down at the weekly farmer's market, buying fresh bread, cheese, pickles and olives for lunch. All things I know my daughter loves. I'd normally buy some nice ham as well but, somehow, I'm off meat these days.

It's Maggie and Stevie's influence, I know. Not that they've ever told me I should stop eating meat, but when I hear Stevie talk about why she doesn't, it makes sense to me. And I love animals. Always have. We had rabbits when the children were little, and we used to have hens, when we lived up there at the old place. I loved the dogs at the Camelford-Bassetts' (I did love the children, too) and the horses, though I was a bit scared of them.

Anyway, I've decided to cut out the meat a bit more, and the fish. But a cake seems acceptable, so on the way back I pop into Bramley's for a small Victoria sponge, which was always Louisa's favourite, and Bramley's do the best in town.

I'm back home by ten, my goods packed away for now, and taking a breather by the window. Needing a breather after a little trip into town is another sure sign of age but I've got to accept these things. Louisa is due at about half-eleven, and she's sent me a text when she's stopped at some services:

Roads are clear and I'm on my way! See you soon, Mum xx

Something about that 'Mum' makes my heart sing. At eleven, I am on my feet, in the kitchen, the kettle on and the radio, too. I have the back door open. It's warming up out there, and I like the sound of the garden birds to filter through into the house.

At 11.28, I hear the sound of a key in the door (I locked it for good measure, so that our visit does not begin with a safety lecture) and I turn to hear my beautiful daughter's voice:

"Hi, Mum!"

Hi, Mum! It's what she'd call when she came in from school; Laurie, too. I've missed it. Missed those days, even though they seemed hard work at the time. Keeping uniforms clean; making sure they both had shoes that fitted; trying to scrape together the money for the occasional school trip; keeping up with homework, and making sure I could understand just what it was my children were learning. I never wanted them to think I was less educated than them, although as it turned out, I'd had a pretty comprehensive education at the non-comprehensive Whiteley School, and I could hold my head high when my children needed help with the majority of their subjects.

I meet Louisa halfway, in the lounge. I'm reminded of my aged shrinking, as my daughter – once the exact same height as me – now appears to tower above me. We both have smiles on our faces; I couldn't stop smiling for anything. We embrace and she kisses my cheek, then tries a surreptitious examination of me, like she's checking for signs of illness, or something. I pretend not to notice.

"It is so nice to see you, Lou," I say. "You look well." She really does. Her dark hair is glossy, and for once a little messy; her cheeks pink and her brown eyes shining.

"I walked down from the hotel," she says. "I thought it made sense to leave the car there."

"Oh, yes, I suppose it does. There's not much in the way of parking round here, that's for sure. Did you have a good journey?"

What do I care about the journey? I mean, I'm glad she's safe, but what I want to know is what is happening in her life. Is she happy? She looks it. I know from experience not to start off with too many questions, though. Hopefully, as we relax in each other's company, the answers will naturally come.

"Would you like a cup of tea?" I ask instead.

"I'd love one, please, Mum. And could we have it in the garden? It's just so nice to be in so much fresh air. I want to make the most of every moment of it."

"Of course we can."

Although I'd planned to save the cake for after lunch, I find myself slicing it now; bringing out a big wedge for my daughter to enjoy with her steaming mug of tea.

"From Bramley's?" she asks, her eyes meeting mine.

"Of course."

"This is too good. Thank you, Mum."

"It's my pleasure." I go inside and get my own mug of tea, and slightly more moderate piece of cake. I'm smiling, still. It's Louisa. Not just seeing her, but seeing her so… happy. Reminding me of her younger days. I don't feel like she's been all that happy recently – not for years, in fact. She loved becoming a mum, but she found it a struggle. I think it was hard for her, as somebody who likes to be in control, suddenly finding that she couldn't be – although she was very, *very* organised and rigid when Ada was little.

So, while motherhood was fulfilling, I always felt like she was living on nervous energy a lot of the time, and constantly fretting about childcare, and her daughter's education. Questioning her own role as a working mum. But Ada has turned out quite delightful, and very much her own person, too. I'd worried a little that Louisa would expect her daughter to follow in her footsteps, but she seems surprisingly relaxed about Ada following her own path in life. And today, she seems surprisingly relaxed, full stop.

I make my own surreptitious maternal appraisal of her as she leans back in the striped sun lounger and closes her eyes in the sun. Her skin looks clear, and her face looks free of the worry lines it sometimes displays. I've worried about her all her life, but never more than since she started work in London; becoming progressively concerned as her career progressed.

She'll tell you she's happy at work, my girl, and she's proud of her accomplishments, as she certainly should be. But it's been stressful, and all-encompassing, and I really don't think it's a healthy way to live, sometimes. Long, late nights in the office, followed by early mornings. I can tell she gets a kick out of it; a buzz, as she'd say. And if I were to ever venture an opinion or voice my concerns, she'd shoot me down. Tell me I wouldn't be saying those things if it was Laurie, not her. Although she should really know that's not my style. It has nothing to do with her gender; it has everything to do with letting her work become her life.

Anyway, it's good to see her now, with the weight off her feet and her shoulders. I'd like to take a walk with her later, around town. Visit some of our favourite old spots. Treat her to an ice-cream. But something stops me from suggesting this. I'm afraid that she'll say she's busy this afternoon.

We sit companionably for a while, watched closely by a gull strutting slowly back and forth across the low roof at the back of the house, its almost orange eyes fixed on us and our plates. It would like to swoop in, I can tell, but this one is not quite brazen enough.

"How are you, Mum? The garden's looking nice."

"I'm really quite well, thank you, love. The garden keeps me busy, and I've been going to the club a bit more."

"Caring the Community?" she grins, and I return her smile. She hates that name as much as I do.

"That's the one. And there's a lovely girl... woman..." I quickly correct myself, knowing Louisa will if I don't, but she's right, really – Maggie isn't a girl, "who volunteers there, and she's taken me out a couple of times, with her daughter."

I find myself playing it down. Not wanting to make too big a deal of my friendship with Maggie. She has been mistaken for my daughter more than once, and stupidly it makes me feel like I've been disloyal to Lou.

"That's really nice," Louisa says, but I feel like she's only half listening. "I'm glad you've got some company, Mum."

There's more to come, I sense, and I keep quiet.

"Actually, Mum," I can see she can barely keep the smile from her face, "I've had some more company lately, too."

"Oh yes?"

"Yes, I've got a… a boyfriend, I suppose."

"Really?" It's been a long time since Louisa has had a boyfriend. I am quite sure she makes the most of the London dating scene that I've read about, but she doesn't tell me anything about that side of things.

"Yes, although we haven't been seeing each other long."

"Well, he must be nice if you're telling me about him."

Her face flushes. "He is nice. He's from work, actually. And you know I don't normally mix work and pleasure. Not when it comes to relationships, anyway."

I do not know this, because she never tells me anything. But I nod, encouragingly, keen to hear more.

"But we get on really well. He came over from America last year, and we've been working closely together, and… we just clicked, I suppose."

"And he is single?" I wince at the stupidity of my own question.

"Mum!" Louisa laughs and I feel relieved that I seem to have got away with that one. "Of course he is. He's been married, no kids. And he's quite a bit younger than me, actually."

"Oh really?" I can't help smiling at this. Go on, Louisa. A toyboy. Why the heck not? "Has Ada met him?"

"No, not yet, but she knows about him."

"And can I ask his name?"

"Yes, he's called AJ. Well, that's not his real name, but everyone at work calls him by his initials, and it seems to suit him, really."

She is gushing, like she used to when she was so much younger, if she'd met a boy on a night out. I used to listen and keep my counsel, knowing that anything which could be construed as negative might mean she wasn't so open in future. But I always kept a close eye on her boyfriends. Found out what I could about them. I didn't want her reliving what I'd put up with from her dad.

"AJ. Sounds very American!"

"I suppose it does, quite! Anyway, strangely enough, he knows this place quite well. He's been seconded to work at our place, but actually works for Canyon Holdings. You know, the place behind the development at the harbour."

"The Saltings? That's quite a coincidence."

"I suppose it is. I couldn't believe it when he was talking about our little town."

I don't mention the fact that she couldn't get away from here fast enough. Or the fact that most of the locals are up in arms about the so-called Saltings.

"He really loves it here. In fact, he might come down this week, too."

That further explains the hotel, then.

"So I'll get to meet him?"

"Maybe," she smiles coyly. It makes me smile, too.

"Louisa," I say. "If he makes you happy, then I already like him. And if he does come down this week, you can bring him here, if you'd like to. Or we can go out, if you'd rather." I don't want to suggest she'd be ashamed of my little home, but I can just imagine rich American AJ working in finance might find the cottage little more than a hovel – or else charming and quaint. I don't know which would be worse.

"I'd like that, Mum," she says.

"Now, shall we have some lunch? And–" I'm just going to say it "– I wondered if you'd like to spend the afternoon with me. I thought we could walk along to the harbour, get a cup of tea and an ice cream somewhere. Just spend some time together." I hope I don't sound too desperate.

"I'd like that, Mum," she says again.

If this is AJ's influence on my daughter, then I really do like him already.

1949

As it happened, Angela was less surprised than Elise might have expected.

She was asleep in front of the dying fire when Elise arrived home, at close to one in the morning. Angela sat up, suddenly, bemused for just a moment, until she shook herself out of it. "Elise, is everything alright?"

"Yes, it's..." How was she going to explain this? How could she? There was no lie she could tell that would pass Angela's knowing, assessing look. "No, not really. Not all, in fact." Elise allowed herself some self-pitying tears, telling Angela exactly what had happened, while the older woman stoked up the fire and filled the kettle.

"I knew it," Angela said. "I knew something like this would happen."

"How? How could you possibly know?"

"I told you before. I've heard rumours – since you've been working there. About *his lordship*," she couldn't keep the sarcasm from her voice, "and the young women who have worked there before. Honestly, Elise, if I'd known before, I would have never suggested you for that job."

So there had been others. Elise's heart sank further still. It wasn't her. She wasn't special. No, this was just what he did. As her mind cast to the children – Charles, Edmond and Tabitha – she stifled a sob. She would not see them again. And what would they think? That she had abandoned them? That she didn't care?

"What a mess," she exclaimed. "What a mess."

"Hush," said Angela. "It's as much of a mess as we let it be. Now listen, you have a place to live, with me, for as long as you want it. And there are other jobs. Better jobs, anyway. Believe me, though I love teaching, if I had my time again, I might have done things differently."

"You still could."

"Bless you, it's nice of you to say, Elise, but I'm a bit long in the tooth to change anything now. But you, you've got your life ahead of you. I'll ask around about work. I'm sure I heard they want a typist at the solicitor's place. You can type, can't you?"

"A bit."

"Well, I can teach you. I've got my dusty old typewriter in my room. We'll get it out tomorrow and spend all day doing it if we have to, and all of Sunday, too. Then Monday, you'll go to the solicitor's and see what they need. Anything they say they want, you can do it, OK?"

Angela's eyes were boring into Elise's, like she was trying to pass on strength that way.

"OK."

"That's my girl. Your mum would be proud. Now, drink your tea, then it's off to bed with you. Get a good night's sleep. Tomorrow's a new day."

"Today."

"Today?"

"Yes, it's Saturday already."

"So it is. Then the rest of your life starts now, OK?"

They sat and sipped in silence, each lost in her own thoughts, letting the heat of the freshly brewed tea flood into them. Elise, shocked yet stoic, took solace from the company of the other woman's strength and determination.

Angela occasionally let her eyes flick to Elise. She had promised Annabel she would look after her, if anything happened, and that is what she intended to do. She could see a shadow of Annabel in Elise, if she looked closely enough, and her stomach clenched along with her jaw, at the gall of that man taking advantage of this girl, and at the loss of the woman she had loved.

Saturday and Sunday were spent on the typewriter, until Elise's wrists ached.

Angela read text after text for Elise to type out as Angela read – using old pieces of Whiteley correspondence from Angela's files ("I won't be needing any of this anymore") and any spare scraps of paper they could find: typing articles and letters from the *Manchester Guardian*; Beatrix Potter's *Peter Rabbit*; the closing acts of *A Midsummer Night's Dream*, sending both Elise and Angela into a reverie, remembering the school production, before the number of girls had dwindled and morale had drooped to a point where a school play seemed neither feasible nor attractive. Elise typed out Robin Puck's lines from memory. It made her feel old.

But by Sunday evening, she was touch-typing. Bored, and exhausted, but nevertheless touch-typing. Her final job, Angela said, was to type up her own curriculum vitae, which was sparse but with Angela's help made Elise sound quite impressive.

"There you go, my girl. Fifty words per minute. Not bad. Not bad, at all."

"I can't believe it! Thank you, Angela. Now I just have to find a job."

"Then tomorrow morning it's straight off to Fawcett's with you. They'll welcome you with open arms, I'm sure of it. A well-educated, well-mannered girl like you. They'd be mad to pass you over."

"I hope you're right."

Angela retired to bed that evening, tired but satisfied. She had succeeded not only in teaching Elise a valuable new skill, but also in keeping her mind off that bloody Lord Whatsisname. She'd heard the rumours about him, of course she had, but weren't they all like that? Men. Well-to-do men, especially. But men in general. Like women owed them something. Now Elise could hold her head high and go out into the world. And yes, she might well end up working for another man. It was almost a given, but in time maybe she'd broaden her knowledge and experience, and find out she didn't have to rely on anyone but herself.

Angela wriggled down under the covers. She felt like Annabel was smiling down on her, from wherever she was. With the sound of the sea whispering in through the open window, she fell into a deep, rich sleep.

In the next room, Elise was not so relaxed. The hours and hours of typing seemed to have rewired her brain and when she closed her eyes she could see a stream of text, line after line, as if imprinted on her eyelids. And then a jolt, as she remembered Friday – which already seemed so long ago. Lord Camelford-Bassett. *Andrew.* The kiss. She touched her lips, where his had been. Remembered the warmth of his mouth and the strange bristling-tickling sensation of his moustache on her skin.

Blood rushed to her face. How could she have allowed that to happen? Why did she want it to happen again? It was wrong, in every way. But the way he had looked at her. The way he had spoken to her. It was like he trusted her, confided in her. She knew he didn't like his life, or his wife, very much. And she imagined him driving down to this little terraced cottage, throwing gravel at her window, her letting him in. Creeping up the stairs...

No. She had to stop thinking like that. And she had to get some sleep. She had to get a job, and would need to be at her best tomorrow morning. Besides, he had let her go, hadn't he? *You're not to bother coming to work on Monday.* If that wasn't a clear enough message, she didn't know what was.

She tossed and turned in her little bed, and knew that sleep would not come. Tiptoeing down the little creaky staircase, she found her shoes and coat in the dark and exited the house through the back door – through the moonlit garden and down the alleyway, which was pitch-black. Crossing the road, she revelled in the silence of the town. The only sound the sea, and the very occasional bad-tempered call of a gull which should really have been asleep.

Down the hill, past the station, and onto the beach. She pulled off her shoes and pressed her bare toes firmly into the cool, damp sand, then walked the length of the beach and back. Breathing slowly, deeply and deliberately. Imagining the air flowing deep into her lungs, and back out again. In time, she felt she could lay her coat down, curl up, and sleep right there, under the stars.

Instead, she trudged back across the soft sand and sat on the edge of the path to shake her shoes and put them back on, then up the hill and across the road, back to bed to sleep at last, soothed by the solitude and peace of her night-time walk.

***

In the morning, Elise walked with Angela part of the way to the school, splitting off to turn right into the town. There it was. Fawcett's Law Firm. With a striking racing-green sign embossed with gold letters. There was a girl standing outside. Elise vaguely recognised her from the dances she'd been to.

"Hello," she said, half-shyly. "Do you work here?"

"Yes, I'm a typist," said the girl, looking Elise up and down. "And you're the one from the school. You work up at the manor, don't you?"

"I do... I did," said Elise. "But I've learned to type now, and I'd like to try office work. I heard there was a job going here." She'd practised that line, about learning to type and office work, and thought it sounded quite authentic.

"Yes, there is. Miss Mablethorpe has gone to be married. Poor bloke," the girl grinned, putting Elise immediately at ease. "I'm Maudie." The girl thrust out her hand.

"Elise." She took Maudie's hand, feeling the girl's soft, warm skin. She realised how much she had missed having a friend her own age, and wondered how Violet was getting on.

They had exchanged letters a few times, Elise making sure to always use the pen that Violet had gifted her. Over time, however, Elise started to feel that she had nothing interesting to tell Violet, who was off furthering her education. Attending lectures and salons and all sorts of things Elise could barely imagine. She knew, really, that Violet would never judge her, but neither would she be stupid enough to fall for the lord of the manor. Not that Elise had necessarily fallen for Lord Camelford-Bassett, but she had at least fallen under his spell. And look where it had got her.

"Mr Fawcett's always late on a Monday morning. He'll be here soon, though. You can ask him about the job then."

The very thought sent Elise's stomach into a bit of a whirl. "What's he like?"

"He's alright," Maudie said, "If you keep him sweet. He can be a bit... friendly."

"Isn't that a good thing?"

"Well. Sort of. He likes young women working for him, I don't think you'll have a problem getting a job."

"I can type fifty words a minute."

"That's very good, but he won't be too worried about that. Honestly, there isn't always a lot of work, and sometimes it's more getting cups of tea for him and his clients. But the pay's OK, and I want to study law myself one day, so I'm trying to learn as much as I can."

"Do you?" Elise was impressed. She still had no idea what she wanted to do. Just earning some money to get by on seemed ambition enough for the time being.

"Yes. I don't suppose it will ever happen, but I want to work in one of the bigger firms, in Penzance or Truro or somewhere. So this seems like a good place to start." Maudie's eyes flicked over Elise's shoulder. "Here he is now."

Elise turned to see a rather portly older man walking down the street behind her, dressed in a tweed suit and with an umbrella hooked over his arm, like a caricature of a London businessman.

"Good morning, Miss Maudie," he said amiably. "And

who do we have here?" His eyes travelled the length of Elise's body and she fought the urge to pull her thin coat tight around her.

"This is Elise, Mr Fawcett," Maudie said. "She's come about the job."

"Oh, yes. Very good, very good. Well, Maudie," he pushed the key into the lock, "you go in and put the heaters on, and the kettle, and I'll take Miss..."

"Morgan," Elise supplied shyly.

"I'll take Miss Morgan into my office."

Maudie raised her eyebrows at Elise behind the man's back. Elise felt at once nervous of this confident, well-spoken man, and warmed by Maudie's friendliness and irreverence. *Please let me get this job*, she thought.

In his office, which was lined with shelves of leatherbound lawbooks, Mr Fawcett hung his umbrella on a tall wooden hatstand, and pulled the blinds at the window, to reveal a view across rooftops and onwards to the sea.

"Lovely view, eh?" Mr Fawcett said. She looked away from the window, to see he was not sharing her line of sight but instead apparently assessing her small bosom. She blushed.

"Now, tell me about yourself, Miss Morgan."

Elise put her CV on her desk. "I typed this last night. I am a keen worker, and did well at school."

"You've just been working up at Tregynon?" Mr Fawcett raised his eyebrows.

"Yes," Elise experienced a little twinge as she thought of the three children. Would they be expecting her this morning? Missing her? She missed them, already. An image of their beach afternoon flashed though her mind.

But she could not think of that.

"I see, and it says here you like acting?"

"Yes, I..." That had been Angela's idea. *You have to show some outside interests.*

"Maybe you'd like to join the town amateur dramatics society. I'm on the committee, you know." His chest puffed out. "And my wife is very keen too. We will be doing *HMS Pinafore* this year. We've had to halt things over the last few years, of course. The war and all that, you know."

The mention of his wife relaxed Elise just a little. "That sounds very good, sir," she said politely.

"Thursday evenings, six till nine, then weekends as well, when we're close to a production. Now, why don't you go downstairs, and Maudie will show you how things work. We'll begin with a two-week trial, two pounds a week, and we'll see how we go, shall we?" He looked at her over the top of his glasses, as his hands began shuffling through some of the papers on his desk.

"I... yes, thank you, sir." Elise stood, unable to believe how easy that had been. Were all job interviews like this? As she turned to go, she was sure she heard him mutter, "Yes, quite a view," to himself. "Shut the door on your way out, there's a good girl," he said more distinctly.

She did as she was bid, then went down the staircase, to the office where Maudie was waiting, bearing a tray with a teapot covered by a cosy, a jug of milk, and a cup and saucer. "For his lordship," she said, rolling her eyes, and the words gave Elise a jolt as she thought once more of her old job. This time last week, she'd had no idea it would be her old job – not so soon, anyway. But here she was. "Did you get it?" Maudie was asking.

"Get it?"

"The job, you ninny."

"Oh! Yes!" Elise smiled. "A two-week trial, anyway."

"That is good news," Maudie said. "Let me take this up to him, then I'll show you your desk, and what we have to do."

"Thank you," said Elise, looking around her. She heard Maudie go up the stairs, and some muffled voices. When the girl returned, she rolled her eyes. "He always insists on me pouring a cup for him, and tries to look down my top."

"He doesn't!"

"Course he does. They're all like that, aren't they? Oh, I suppose you don't know, what with being at an all-girls' school, but believe me, once boys are out of short trousers, all they're interested in is trying to get a look, or cop a feel."

"Oh."

"I wouldn't worry about it! That's just life, isn't it? Tell you what, you want to come to the dance with me on Saturday. Davey'll be there, and some of his friends. They're not bad boys. Not all of them, anyway."

"Is Davey your boyfriend?"

"We've been walking out a while now."

"Less chatting, more working, girls!" Mr Fawcett's voice boomed down the stairs.

Maudie whispered, "He loves doing that. Reckon it makes him feel powerful, up in his turret, with his girls below him doing all his work. Come on, though, we'd better show willing."

Elise's desk was next to Maudie's, but Maudie had the view from the window. "I started in your desk," she said, "then when Miss Mablethorpe left, I took her place here.

Sorry, but you have to work your way up to this seat!"

It didn't matter to Elise at all. She had her own desk, and a typewriter. She felt suddenly very grown up.

"We start with the correspondence," Maudie said. "Here, I've got a pile for you. I'll show you what to do."

Elise listened carefully as Maudie went through the different types of letters, and the stamp to be applied to each one. Every now and then one was deemed 'urgent' and put into a special pile, to go straight up to Mr Fawcett. "I'll take them up today," Maudie said, "give you a day's grace from his perviness."

It also gave Elise a moment to take it all in. A new job, and a new friend, she hoped. An invite to a dance, and an invitation to join the local theatre group, which she thought Angela might like, at least. She allowed herself a quick glance back to the previous week and marvelled at how much had changed, her feet having hardly had time to touch the ground.

As the days of her first week in her new job passed, Elise found her feet in her role, and learned a few tricks to avoid getting too close to Mr Fawcett, too.

"Tried and tested," Maudie said. "Sometimes he'll come and stand behind your chair, supposedly to look over your work, but more like to look down your top. Cross your arms over your chest. Higher up, see, otherwise you're just pushing your boobs up. Like this."

Maudie folded her arms across her chest, with her hands almost in her armpits. "Stand behind me, can you see anything?"

"Er... no," Elise did as she was told, still slightly in awe of her worldly new friend. She stood behind her, looking down, but could see only Maudie's arms.

"You lean back, so he can look at your typing, but with your arms crossed, he can't see anything. Only, be careful not to lean back too far, or you'll be leaning into him, right... there." She raised her eyebrows knowingly. "Pull your chair in close to the desk."

"Is he really that bad?" Elise asked. Mr Fawcett had been friendly to her, and seemed to want her to feel at ease in her new workplace.

"Trust me. I mean, he's not a horrible man. He's quite nice to work for, and at Christmas he gave me two pounds' bonus, but he's still an old perv."

This was a whole new world for Elise. Work. Men. Would she ever feel as at ease with it all as Maudie seemed to? But then Maudie had brothers, too, and had gone to school with boys. She seemed to know it all, and Elise felt very young and naïve in her presence.

"You're coming to the dance tomorrow, aren't you?" Maudie asked Elise on Friday afternoon.

"I... yes, that would be nice." She was nervous at the prospect, but knew she would have to push herself. Besides, after just five days with Maudie, she felt like she already had a friend for life. Was that silly, after a week? They had clicked immediately, despite their difference in experience, and Elise didn't think she had ever laughed so much. She loved Violet dearly, but Violet was a little more serious and studious than Maudie, whose main aim in life seemed to be to have fun.

"I'll have to meet you there. At the hall; you know, the only place in town that a dance could possibly be held. I'll be there at half-seven."

"I'll see you there."

She would have preferred to have been going with Maudie, Elise thought, as she readied herself for the dance. She had only two dresses for work, which she wore on alternate days, and one 'better' dress, which she had washed and pressed, dressed only in her slip and bra.

"Not in the front room," Angela had scolded. "You never know who might look through the window." She had pulled the curtains half to, then sent Elise upstairs. "I'll finish this."

"Thank you," Elise said.

Angela was in a good mood, because she had gone along to the amateur dramatics society on Thursday evening. Elise had decided not to, in the end. Maudie may have had something to do with that decision.

"Why choose to spend more time with Mr F than you have to? You're not getting paid to do am dram, are you?"

"No," Elise conceded, though she felt like it was a bit of an insult to Mr Fawcett to decline his invitation.

Angela, however, had been more than happy to go. "I'll say hello to him from you," she said. "And tell him to keep his hands off you."

Elise had ended up telling Angela about her new boss, and the things Maudie said.

"Don't!" Elise had exclaimed, horrified at the thought.

"As if I would!" Angela had laughed.

So the town players had a new member, albeit not one Mr Fawcett could, or would even want to, get his hands on. And Elise had a new friend, and the green shoots of a social life.

It was a warm evening as she walked into town, aware of glances from passers-by. Faces were becoming familiar, she realised, since she had lived in the town for a few months now. Perhaps she would soon be an accepted face, too. Gulls were shrieking on rooftops, and wheeling overhead as she walked down to the harbour. The tide was in, water slapping against the walls, the fishing fleet returning to offload their hauls.

Elise felt a sudden, unexpected, and unfamiliar, sense of joy. Freedom. The world opening out in front of her in a way she had not imagined.

She had missed the three children this last week, but she had not missed the manor house, or the stifling situation of working in somebody's home. Instead, she was in an office, with a colleague her own age, and a lunch break. And now here she was, going to a Saturday night dance. She felt quite cosmopolitan.

As she drew nearer to the hall, however, nerves took over. Should she wait outside for Maudie, or go in? She wished she had thought to ask. The smiling lady on the door drew here in, though. "Hello, dear, are you coming in?"

"Yes, I'm meant to be meeting a friend here."

"Well, come in, come in. The band's just warming up."

Sure enough, Elise could hear the sound of real musical instruments being tested out, behind a wall of excited chatter. She paid her entry fee and followed the sounds, finding a chair at the edge of the hall, where she could sit while she waited for Maudie, if she wasn't already here.

The clock on the wall showed it was approaching quarter-to-eight and there was still no sign of Maudie. The band was playing the second tune of the night, and Elise jumped as a boy appeared in front of her. "Want a dance?" he smiled.

His smiling face was lightly tanned, his nose scattered with a few darker freckles and his teeth white and straight. It was the boy she had seen at the dances when she'd come with Violet.

Elise looked around. "Who, me?"

"Yes, you!" he laughed. "Who else?"

"I'm... I'm waiting for a friend." She had to speak loudly to make herself heard.

The boy leaned in, "I'm waiting for somebody, too. We can wait together. But we might as well dance while we're waiting."

He was a good dancer, and Elise soon lost her inhibitions. She had always loved dancing, but had not had too many opportunities to dance with a boy before.

The tune ended and the band began playing *Paper Doll*. It began slowly and he pulled her closer, smiling at her and holding her gaze while they moved around the floor. She was aware that they were attracting some attention, and decided that at the end of this tune she would politely return to her seat.

"Oh," he said, though, the band still in full swing. "She's here." He dropped Elise's hand, which he'd taken to twirl her around as the tune had picked up speed. She had turned to look in the same direction as him. Her stomach dropped.

"Maudie," she said.

Her new friend was looking at her and her dance partner, and not looking particularly happy. It was the boy she was glaring at, though, not Elise. The other dancers on the floor moved around the trio, all pretending not to be paying any attention to the scene playing out in front of them.

"I see you've met Davey," Maudie said to Elise.

"I... I had no idea."

"No, I realise that." Maudie put a hand briefly on Elise's arm. "Come on," she said, turning her back on the boy, and pulling Elise with her to the drinks table. "Don't worry," she said, "I know what he's like."

"Honestly," Elise said, "I had no idea. I promise. I was about to come and sit down, anyway."

She wanted to say more, that he had asked her, and wouldn't really take no for an answer.

"It's fine," her friend said, "honestly." But she didn't look like it was fine. "That's Davey for you. I knew I should have gone with Fred instead, and now he won't go near me, for fear of upsetting Davey."

Elise said nothing. She had no idea who Fred was, and she was just feeling angry at herself for allowing another stupid situation to happen. Was this what it was like, when men were involved? Or boys, in this case. Her experience with the opposite sex was very slim so far, but none of it was positive.

"Let's me and you dance together, Elise!" Maudie had exclaimed all of a sudden, putting her cup down on a windowsill. She grabbed Elise's hand, allowing her just enough time to put her own drink down, then pulled her onto the floor.

Elise was just pleased that it seemed she had not ruined her friendship before it had even had a chance to start, and she whirled around the floor with Maudie, until their faces were red, and they were out of breath.

"Ha! That gave him something to look at," Maudie said, her eyes fixed on Davey, who was skulking at the side of the hall with a few other boys his age. She finished her drink and left Elise standing alone, then marched right over to him. Elise could not hear what was being said, but she noticed the other boys edging away. Davey looked shocked, then annoyed, and pulled himself up to his full height, but Maudie did not give way. She stomped back across the dance floor to Elise.

"That's told him."

"What did you say to him?" Elise was in awe of her friend once more.

"I told him it was over. That he's a flirt and a cheat. And a bully."

"A bully?"

"Yes, well he would be if I let him."

Elise risked a glance across the hall. She was shocked to see Davey send a smile her way. How dare he? She was outraged on her friend's behalf, and determined to look past those white teeth and freckles.

Over the evening, her new friend introduced her to some of the other local girls and boys, who were friendly with her. Having Maudie on her side seemed to give her automatic approval and by the time the dance ended, Elise felt – if not part of things here – as though she might become a part of them, over time.

She said goodbye to Maudie on the corner, as her friend's house was at the other side of town, then walked off into the warm, still night, alone. Opting to retrace her steps back down by the harbour, the thick, humid air glittering her skin with salt. If she licked her lips, she could taste it.

She was tired now, from all the dancing and laughing, and making conversation with people she didn't know. It had been lovely, but exhausting, and she was looking forward to a quiet Sunday at home. She just had some washing to do, and a book she was looking forward to finishing.

"Hey," she heard a voice behind her. "It's Eliza, isn't it?"

"Elise," she corrected automatically, as she turned to see Davey a few steps away. How had she not heard him before now?

"Elise," he said, "sorry."

She turned and carried on walking. Not wishing to appear rude, but not wanting to betray her new friend, either.

"Sorry about this evening," he said, catching up with her. "With Maudie, I mean. I was going to end things with her tonight anyway."

"Well, perhaps you should have done that before asking somebody else to dance," Elise said primly.

"You're right, I should," he said, and she was wrong-footed by his honesty. "I should. But you looked a bit lonely, all on your own. And I always wanted to ask you to dance; before, you know, when you used to come with your friend from the school."

So he remembered her. And he knew who she was, or at least that she was from Whiteley. Elise was flattered. But her loyalty was to her friend. She didn't know what to say.

"Can I walk you home? I have to pass your house anyway."

He even knew where she lived. But then, it was that kind of town, she thought. He was probably related to the people who had lived there before her and Angela. Everyone was related here, or so it seemed sometimes.

"If you like," she said stiffly. She hated to appear rude,

but had no idea what to say, and no intention of leading him on.

"Don't sound too enthusiastic!" he said, but he laughed. And she couldn't help smiling.

"So I can make you smile," he said. "Well, that's good. I thought you hated me."

"I don't hate anyone."

They walked quietly for a few steps.

"Maudie's finished with me," he said.

"I know."

"So I'm free to go out with whoever I choose."

"Good for you."

"I'd like to choose you."

"You can't just choose me. Don't I have any say in the matter?"

"Well yes, of course," he said.

"Then I say no," Elise carried on walking, not looking at him.

"But why?"

"You know why."

"Maudie ended things with me, not the other way round."

"But it was your behaviour that prompted it."

"Not true. Well, not entirely true. She's fond of Fred Fishwick."

"That's not a real name!" Elise couldn't help laughing.

"It is! I swear it, we were all at school together. Fred. You ask her. Ask Maudie."

She had mentioned a Fred, Elise remembered. Then she also remembered Maudie saying Davey was a bully. He didn't seem like a bully, though. Persistent, yes, but that wasn't the same thing, was it?

But then, hadn't Maudie marched across that dance floor, and given him what for? Maybe Davey wasn't the only one with a temper.

Whatever, it didn't matter. Elise was not about to become involved with her friend's recently discarded boyfriend. Not when she had only known Maudie a week, and Maudie had been so much fun, and so generous with her, inviting her out and introducing her to all her friends. Why on earth would Elise risk all that?

Elise

On the first evening, Louisa is tired. She'd suggested we go out for a meal, but I can see her stifling a yawn. We are back at my house. *Our house*, I think, although at some point it has become less a family home, and I wonder fleetingly when that transition took place.

We've had a lovely afternoon, wandering around town, and sitting for quite some time on one of the harbour benches, on the opposite side to the development, where the building work continues regardless of the weekend. There is never silence, even on a Sunday – not at the moment, as if it would slow the momentum.

"Why don't you just get an early night tonight, love? All this sea air gets you like that. We can eat out tomorrow. I'm a bit tired myself, in all honesty."

I can still read my daughter like a book, and I can tell this idea appeals to her, but she doesn't want to seem too keen, for fear of hurting my feelings. "Are you sure?"

"Quite sure. Really, go and treat yourself to an early night in your lovely hotel bed. You'll wake up to the sound of gulls and the sea in the morning, and you can come here whenever you're ready. After breakfast, or even before. I can do us eggs if you like."

"That does sound good, Mum. Can I text you in the morning? I'd quite like to sleep in if I can."

"Of course. You make the most of it. We've got all week."

"I love you, Mum," she says, and I feel my heart swell like the sea.

I actually need a bit of time to reflect, and think things through. It seems AJ's influence on my daughter is far-reaching, and he's encouraged her to find out more about her background. Specifically, about her dad.

Louisa was just about eighteen months when Davey died. I don't suppose she remembers a thing about him, and I suspect, well, I know, that I have never been particularly forthcoming with details about him. Laurie, too, remains tight-lipped on the subject, and I don't know if it's because he's forgotten Davey on purpose, or if those memories, untended and certainly not encouraged, have withered away.

Now, Louisa wants to know. Says she thinks it might help her feel more complete. Which sounds like a load of American claptrap to me, quite frankly, but maybe she's right.

The question is, what to tell her? *Your dad was a bastard?* I don't think she needs that.

Also, when to tell her? I don't want to do it before AJ's visit. I can imagine her telling him everything and I feel, well, embarrassed, that I was ever so stupid to be with somebody like Davey. And I know, I know, it wasn't stupid, and I would never call somebody else stupid for being in that situation. But still, she's bound to tell him, and I'd rather it be after we meet for the first time.

I'm planning to mull it over tonight, when, despite the fact that I genuinely am tired, I'll head out to the beach in the dark. I do my best thinking during those night-time walks. I just hope I don't bump into Louisa. But I am quite sure she'll be tucked up between immaculate white sheets, dreaming of handsome Americans; or one, at the very least.

***

On Sunday morning, I wake late, and remember immediately that my daughter is in town. I check the time and see it's well past eight. I hope that Louisa is having that lie-in she wanted, but what if she's on her way to see me? I promised her breakfast, as I recall. I ease my aching bones from the bed. Yesterday, I did a lot more walking than I'm used to these days. And last night's walk was a little harder than normal. I was ambushed by rain moving swiftly in when I was on the beach. Walking home was a case of head-down, best-foot-forward, rain dripping from my hood so that my face was streaked with the sky's tears.

Straight out of my wet clothes when I got in, though even this is more effort these days; having to lean on the back of a chair to pull off my socks and my trousers, involuntarily groaning with the effort. I could feel my cheeks beginning to glow in the dry warmth of the house and I'd had the foresight to put pyjamas on the radiator, and an extra hour on the boiler. Easing into my warm nightclothes while the kettle boiled, it was not long before I was upstairs in bed, thinking of my daughter just up the hill; outside the town, but so very close.

And I'd made a decision, to be honest – more or less – and tell her just what her dad was like.

1949

All around, the air was heating up, in the depths of the summer. Somewhere close, at her shoulder, was Annabel. Always. A neatly packed box Elise chose not to open too often, bursting with memories both painful and sweet. The love never went away, Elise had realised. It was real, and almost tangible. It felt like her heart had cracked down the middle when she thought about her mum. It seemed like Angela wanted to talk about Annabel sometimes, but Elise often felt she was not the right person to listen. Clearly, Angela had cared deeply about her mum, and it was slowly dawning on Elise just how deeply. She wasn't sure how she felt about any of it. Fold it up, put it in the box, to be unpacked at a later date – or maybe never.

At work, Maudie was her usual self, and Fred Fishwick had asked her to the next dance, which was another week away.

"Are you coming, Elise?"

"Me?" Elise had not thought Maudie would ask her again, not after what had happened with Davey. "Well, yes, I suppose so."

"Don't sound too excited!" Maudie grinned.

"It's not that, it's just…"

"Davey. I know. Don't you worry about him. But if I were you, I'd steer clear of him. He's bad news, that one."

Elise pictured the boyish tan, the freckles, the white teeth. He didn't really look like bad news to her. Still, she should take Maudie's word for it. After all, her friend knew these people, and she didn't.

"Thank you, Maudie, and I'm sorry again about…"

"Don't say another word! You weren't to know, and it did me a favour, really."

"Well, if you're sure…" Elise said doubtfully.

"I am. Now, not another word, you hear? But if you're sensible, you'll listen to me about Davey Plummer. There are plenty of other nice boys around, and you're like an exotic animal to them."

"I don't think I want to be an animal of any sort!" Elise laughed.

"You know what I mean. But Davey, he's…"

"Girls! Less chatter, more work!" boomed Mr Fawcett from upstairs. "Do I have to come down and take you in hand?"

It was meant as a joke, of sorts, but Maudie and Elise both looked at each other and shuddered. They turned back to their typewriters, Maudie's head full of happy thoughts of Fred, Elise's a confused mixture of Davey Plummer and Lord Camelford-Bassett, and what to wear to the dance.

Maudie had the answer to that one, though. As the girls ate their meagre sandwiches leaning against the old stone wall of the churchyard, in the shade of an ash tree, she looked at Elise.

"Shall we switch dresses for Saturday? You wear one of mine, and I'll wear one of yours. It'll be like something new, for each of us. We're about the same size, too."

Elise looked at her taller friend.

"I know, I've a couple of inches on you, but I can pin up the hem, and let yours down, if it's got any give. Do you think it has?"

Her face shone with excitement, making Elise laugh.

"I think it probably has. Otherwise, it's going to be a bit

short. You'll have the town talking about you!"

"Why don't I come over on Saturday? There's too many boys at my house. We can get ready together."

"I'd love that."

So it was, on the Saturday, Elise and Maudie were giggling together in the front room of 8 Godolphin Terrace, Maudie with pins in her mouth (you try giggling with pins in your mouth, it's not easy), as Elise stood on a chair, patiently waiting for her friend to adjust the hem. The dress was a little loose on her, too, but it was just a pleasure to be in something new and different.

Maudie had examined Elise's dresses and found the one with the longest hem, which she unpicked and neatened up with great skill.

"I wish I could do that," Elise said admiringly.

"You can. I'll show you how some day."

"Not today, though."

"No, not today."

Maudie stayed for an early tea, sitting and chatting easily with Angela. It was something else Elise admired in her friend, and envied to a degree: her sense of ease with other people; strangers. Elise felt shy and awkward much of the time.

They'd had very different upbringings. Maudie, in a large family, with lots of uncles, aunts and cousins nearby, was cheerful and sociable, whereas Elise favoured close, one-to-one friendships. But she loved Maudie's good humour, and was determined to learn from her new friend.

The girls walked to the hall together, the direct way. Elise had suggested going along by the harbour.

"What do you want to do that for?" asked Maudie. To her, Elise supposed, the harbour had just always been there. It was a fact of life, and nothing particularly special. For Elise, it was still a novelty, living in this little town with its active fishing fleet. She loved to see the boats and, occasionally, the seal that would pop its head above the deep green sea, looking for soft-hearted fishermen to fix with its round, shining eyes.

"Let's just get to the dance, shall we? Fred will be waiting."

If Elise had worried she would be a wallflower while her friend danced with Fred, she need not have worried. Tonight, as the band played, she had a choice of partners. Good-natured local boys, who were keen to take her around the dance floor, showing off their skills. Now and then, she would pass Maudie and Fred, who stayed true to each other all night long.

Tired from all the dancing, Elise took a break, hoping to catch Maudie's eye so they could stop and have a drink together. However, Maudie and Fred were nowhere to be seen. She leaned against the wall, feeling suddenly self-conscious and vulnerable. There was nobody here she really knew. She decided that she would wait five minutes, and then look outside.

The band struck up again and one of her previous partners, a tall blond-haired boy, came to ask her to dance, but she smiled and shook her head. The excitement of the evening had worn off and, with no Maudie to chat to, all Elise wanted now was to go home.

A group of girls Elise recognised were gathered just outside the doorway. "Have you seen Maudie?" Elise asked. They shook their heads.

"Actually, I think I saw her go down there with Fred," one of them gestured towards a dark alley, and raised her eyebrows knowingly.

"Sounds like Maudie," one of the others said, and the group laughed meanly.

Elise didn't know what to say. Should she wait for Maudie, or would her friend be too wrapped up in her new romance now? Elise waited at the corner of the hall for a while, but the street remained empty, and the gaggle of girls had gone back inside. Dejected, Elise decided to walk home.

Her footsteps rang in the dark, empty streets, and she felt suddenly very alone. She imagined she could hear Maudie's laugh, and Fred's voice murmuring, but she pushed the thought away. It was just in her head.

Then she remembered the harbour. Why should she not walk that way now, with no Maudie to put her off, she thought stubbornly. It was her choice. Her Saturday night. She took a left turn that would bring her down to the harbour front, her senses brought alive by a whisk of fresh air, full of the scent of salt and fish and seaweed. A loose paper danced along the floor and Elise's skirt blew suddenly. She smoothed it down, glad that there was nobody there to see. As the street opened onto the harbour front, she stopped. There was a figure standing on the harbourside. A man. There was something unnerving about being in the dark, with an unknown man close by and nobody else around. Should she turn back and walk home the other way?

No, she reasoned. Just because it was a man, and it was dark, it didn't mean there was any danger. It just felt... uncomfortable. But she had wanted to walk down by the harbour, and why shouldn't she do just that? She had walked on the beach alone the other night, and it had been liberating.

She stepped out, more confidently than she felt, and the man turned. Only, it wasn't a man – not quite. A boy of her own age, and one that she recognised. Davey. She had noticed his absence at the dance, and been relieved. Now here he was, looking straight at her.

"Hello," he smiled. "We must stop meeting like this. Have you been at the hall?"

"Yes." She felt prim and purse-lipped.

"Good evening, was it? I don't suppose it was, if you've left already."

"It was, as it happens. But I just wanted some fresh air. And I'm tired."

"And Maudie spent all night with Fred Fishwick, I suppose?"

"That's none of your business," said Elise.

"I suppose not. But I'm right, aren't I?"

He'd come closer to her and in the dark of the night, his eyes were like deep pools. "Shall I walk you home?" he suggested, affably. "You shouldn't be down here, all alone. Might get mistaken for a lady of the night."

Elise was not completely naïve and could guess what he meant by this, she thought. But equally, perhaps this was a term for a mythical sea creature? A mermaid, maybe. She certainly wasn't going to ask him to clarify.

"I'm fine," she said stiffly. "I shall be walking straight home, and it isn't far."

"It's on my way, though, as you know, so no harm in me walking you, is there? I'll make sure you get back safely. It was alright last time, wasn't it? I didn't bite."

There was no arguing, really. It would seem silly to be walking the same way but metres apart.

"Alright then," she said.

"Don't sound too excited!" he laughed, and she thought of Maudie saying much the same when she'd suggested the dance. How she wished she was with her friend now. But Maudie had left her behind, she remembered. Sloped off down that alley with Fred Fishwick, if those girls were to be believed.

Davey fell into step beside her. "So, are you staying, then?"

"Staying?"

"Yes, in Cornwall. You're from London, aren't you?"

"Yes, I... well, that seems a long time ago." She didn't want to be flattered that he knew this about her, but she was. Had he been asking around?

"Are your parents there?"

"No, they're both dead."

"I'm sorry." He sounded like he really was.

"It's alright. There are a lot of dead people these days." What a stupid thing to say. She was glad he couldn't see her face flush with embarrassment.

"And there's only going to be more," he said.

"This is a cheerful conversation!" she tried smiling, and couldn't help but feel gratified when he returned the look.

"You're right. Straight in the deep end, eh? I'm glad you're staying, though."

She said nothing to this, and was annoyed at how pleased she felt. *He's bad news, that one*. Maudie's words came back to her. Was he? He certainly seemed friendly enough, and thoughtful, too. Could it be that her friend was warning her off because she still liked him? Elise thought of how willingly Maudie had gone off with Fred Fishwick; it was quite shocking, really. So who was Maudie to dish out advice when it came to boys?

"And you like your new job?"

"Yes, I… It's interesting."

"Well, that's good."

"Do you have a job, Davey?"

"Yes, I do, *Elise*." He grinned as he used her name and she thought how she liked the sound of it from his mouth; his slightly rounded accent rolled the letters across his tongue.

"What do you do?"

"I work for my dad. He's a fish merchant. Used to be a fisherman, now he's a go-between. I'm meant to be learning his trade."

"And do you like it?"

"No!" he laughed. "But I'm to think myself lucky, not having to go out on the boats, and being too young to have gone to war."

Elise understood he was quoting somebody else; his father, perhaps?

"Not so lucky that my dad's a drinker and he's quick with his fists."

Elise felt shocked, again. Could this be true? She knew there would be people like that out there – but this happening in real life, to somebody she knew? She felt suddenly very sorry for the boy walking next to her.

"Does he… does he hit you?"

"And the rest," Davey stopped, and looked at her. "I shouldn't have said anything. You won't tell anyone, will, you, Elise?"

"I won't. I swear."

They were nearing Godolphin Terrace and Elise realised she didn't want the walk to end. Besides, she had wanted to go to the beach. But she couldn't suggest that to Davey. He might get the wrong idea.

"Good. Thank you. You're easy to talk to."

"And you are, too."

He smiled quickly at her. "Will you come to the next one with me?"

"The next what?" she asked – dimly, she realised.

"The next dance. Be my partner."

"I'd like that," she answered truthfully, although part of her was worried as to what Maudie would say when she found out. But she had made her bed with Fred Fishwick now, and she would just have to accept that Elise was going with Davey.

"Didn't you listen when I warned you about him?" Maudie sighed despairingly.

"Well, you went with him," Elise said, defensively.

"Exactly, and that's how I know. Oh, I know he's good looking, and charming, and plays the sympathy card beautifully, but you watch out for that temper of his. I mean it."

Could it really be that the young man who had walked her home and bid her goodnight, without so much as trying to touch her; the boy who had confided to her his family troubles, was the same untrustworthy, bad-tempered boy Maudie described?

But then, he had asked her to dance when he should have been waiting for Maudie. And hadn't he winked at her, all those months ago, when she was still at school? Elise was torn, between her friend and the feelings she was developing for Davey. She didn't want to believe those bad things of him; that was the truth of the matter. And maybe he and Maudie were just not suited to each other.

She didn't wish to be disloyal to her friend, but she was less than impressed by what had happened on the night of the dance.

"Where did you get to on Saturday night, Maudie?" Elise changed the subject. "I looked for you and Fred, but you were nowhere to be seen."

"I know, I know, I'm sorry. He wasn't well. I had to get him outside, then take him home. I came back as quick as I could, but you'd left already."

Now Elise was confused. She didn't know what to believe, but she couldn't very well go accusing Maudie of behaving disreputably.

"I didn't know where you were. And I didn't know anybody else there, so I went home. That's when I saw Davey, by the harbour."

"Contemplating jumping in, was he?" Maudie sighed. "Look, Elise, I don't want to sound like I'm trying to put you off him."

"But you are."

"Well, yes, I am. He's a nice boy, in some ways, but he's troubled. And believe you me, if you get close to somebody who's troubled, you take on their troubles. You know the saying, a problem shared is a problem halved?"

"Yes, I've heard it."

"It's not true. Not where Davey is concerned. A problem shared is a problem doubled. Just… well, do as you wish. Go to the dance with him, but be careful, OK?"

It felt like Maudie was giving her permission to go to

the dance, which did not sit well with Elise. Who was she to tell her what to do?

"I will," she said. "And you be careful with Fred, too."

"What do you mean?" Maudie asked, looking annoyed herself now.

"Just. What people were saying about you."

"What were they saying?"

Elise wished she had kept her mouth shut.

"That you'd gone off down the alley with him."

"Who said that? No, don't tell me, I can guess. And you believed them?"

"I didn't know what to think."

"Well. I've told you what happened, it's your choice whether you listen to me, about Fred and about Davey. Your choice entirely."

The rest of the day was spent in a frosty atmosphere, to the point that Elise was actually glad when Mr Fawcett came downstairs with his usual inappropriate behaviour.

"You two haven't fallen out, have you? It's very quiet down here. I thought I'd better come and make sure you're both being good girls," he looked at them both in turn. "Now, we can't have arguments in the workplace, can we? I'll have to put you over my knee if you can't get on."

This remark did at least break the ice between the girls, who looked at each other in mutual disgust.

"No problem here, Mr Fawcett," Maudie said. "We're both just a bit tired, that's all."

"I hope you haven't been having too much fun," their boss said with a leer over the top of his glasses.

The remark hit a bit of a raw nerve after what Elise

had said to Maudie, and she was keen to move things on. "Oh, no, just the usual housework, and Maudie's been looking after her cousins."

"Well, those young tearaways will keep you on your toes, Miss Branigan."

"Yes, sir. They certainly do."

"Make sure you get a good night's sleep tonight, eh? Can't have my girls all bleary-eyed and bad-tempered. You're the bright spot in my day, you know."

When he left the office, Elise and Maudie rolled their eyes at each other and Maudie pretended to be sick. Disgusting as Mr Fawcett's attentions were, they had at least got the girls' friendship back on a more even footing.

Elise

For each day of Louisa's visit, she sleeps in, or so she tells me. I have a sneaking suspicion that she also spends a bit of time checking her work emails, as she lets something slip one day:

"I'm going to have a lot to do next week."

"I'm sure. Try and put it out of your mind this week, though." I am well aware that I sound like somebody who has no idea how it all works. And, to be fair, I've never had a job like hers, but I have worked hard in my life, and I did have a career of my own, of sorts. Not that Louisa would see it that way. Running a small-town solicitor's office.

How all-consuming this job of hers is, and has been for all the years she's worked in it. But when she began, they were two separate entities. Now, I feel like they're entwined, like weed in fishing nets. I want her to know, though, that I do get it – I see how much her life and her work are as one. I just can't help wishing that she could put it away for a week.

"It's not that easy, Mum," I sense the irritation in her, but she keeps it in check. We are both on our best behaviour this week.

"I know, I'm sorry. I don't suppose it's that easy to just forget about it. It's a shame you haven't got two weeks down here. I always think it takes a week to unwind, before you can really feel like you're relaxed."

"Two weeks would be lovely, but it's just not... Tim says there's a meeting on Monday that I won't even have prepared for, unless I work over the weekend."

"You've heard from Tim, then?" Tim is her personal assistant, and I must admit it appeals to me, this different balance of power between the sexes.

"Oh, err, yes, I... anyway, like you said, better to try and put it out of my mind. I'll just have to work late on Sunday."

"That's a shame," I say, but I leave it at that. It's her life. Her work. She needs to do what she needs to do. "I'm proud of you, Louisa." The words are out of my mouth before I've considered them, and I realise how easy it was to say. And how I could have said it so many times before.

"Are you?" She looks up at me, and I feel my whole diaphragm squeeze in. It's as if my child is looking at me, from fifty – make that sixty – years ago. Has it really taken me this long to tell her? Surely I must have told her so before. Maybe I assumed she knew I was. "Yes, my darling, I'm really proud of you, and I always have been. God knows, I have no idea what you actually do—" she laughs at this "– but bloody hell, Lou, you obviously do it well."

I want to add that I wish she'd look after herself, but this would definitely extract any of the magic from the moment.

"Thank you, Mum," she says softly, and she hugs me. We are down by the harbour, with quite a few people passing on foot and in cars, but my daughter is hugging me tightly, in public, and I think this has been a long time coming, too. I feel small in her embrace, but I still feel the strong one; the protector. I hold her firmly, trying to transmit all my warmth; my strength; my love for her.

The day that follows is maybe my favourite of the whole week. We don't do a lot. We go from the harbour to Bramley's, and sit in the window, eating doughnuts and sharing a pot of tea.

After this, we visit the charity bookshop and pick up some great finds. She is, unusually, in the mood for some light reading, and buys a trio of holiday romances. I can't help thinking this is also to do with AJ, whose visit is now imminent. He will be here tomorrow, and I can't pretend I'm not keen to meet him. I, meanwhile, get a couple of du Mauriers, which I've read before but had passed on to charity at some point. I am keen to read them again.

We take them back to my house, and we sit for some time, companionably, reading our new books. Having said that, I am finding it hard to concentrate; preferring to sneak glances at my beautiful girl, and just to drink it in. The quiet, broken only by the ticking of the clock, and the turning of pages. I don't want to break the spell.

Later, we take a walk on the beach before tea, and Louisa cooks for me; a mackerel salad, followed by a delicious lemon meringue pie. This is followed by a video call with Ada and Laurie, which is a real treat, although Laurie keeps cutting out and his face freezes in all manner of unfortunate expressions. It makes me feel like my small family is pulled tight together, no matter how far apart we are. I want to suggest we do this regularly, but a part of me is worried that they won't be so keen; or they'll be too busy.

I do, however, venture, "Wouldn't it be nice if we could all be together in person? Before too long."

"That would be amazing, Gran," Ada's beautiful young

face smiles on the screen.

"I'd be up for that," Laurie says, surprising me.

"Me too," says Louisa.

"Really?"

"Of course, Gran!" Ada laughs. "What about the summer? Or Christmas?"

Christmas sounds a long time away, but I know by now how fast things come round.

"I could do Christmas," Laurie says.

"I'm sure I can, too. And in the meantime, Mum," Louisa smiles at me, "I'll be back more often. I plan to do this far more regularly."

I'm no idiot, and I know that AJ is also a reason for these visits. I gather he'll be spending more time here as the Saltings really begins to take shape, but who cares? The main thing is, she'll be here.

We end the call with promises to make plans for Christmas, and me fretting about where to put them all, but I know better than to say anything. They will laugh my worries away – affectionately, perhaps, but it will still make me feel belittled. We will work it out, anyway.

Louisa and I have a small whisky nightcap and then she's hugging me – "I love you, Mum," and whirling out of the door into the still, dark night. I can feel her anticipation at the advent of AJ's visit. And I share it, too. What with the prospect of more visits from her, and more days out with Maggie and Stevie, life somehow doesn't feel quite as empty as it used to.

1950

It began with curtailing her friendship with Maudie. Davey and Elise had been going out for a while when she mentioned to him that she and Maudie intended to spend Saturday together, working on some new dresses – new to them, at least. Maudie had been given some old clothes of her aunt's and was keen to get to work adjusting them for her own use. She had offered one to Elise as well, and promised to help her learn how to take it in and up.

"You're not to spend too much time with her, Elise. She's not a good influence."

"Who? Maudie?" Elise had asked, shocked.

"Yes. Miss Branigan," Davey said, grimly. "You know she's got a reputation around town?"

"What kind of reputation?" Elise said, bristling but not being quite able to push away thoughts of Maudie and Fred down that alleyway.

"I think you know what I mean," Davey said, his smiling mouth fixed in a short, tight line. "Don't play the innocent with me."

Elise felt her trademark cheek-flush and was annoyed at herself for reacting. And annoyed at Davey for saying these things. What did he mean, about not playing the innocent?

He touched her face. "Sorry, my love, I didn't mean to embarrass you."

I'm not embarrassed, Elise thought, but she was just glad he was being nice to her again. Smiling at her. He leaned forward to kiss her, and she let him. She was still getting used to this physical side of a relationship, as much as she was to being attached to somebody.

Angela didn't seem too keen, which Davey had picked up on. "She's just jealous," he said. "Probably wants you for herself."

This made Elise feel uncomfortable, given her growing understanding of the relationship her mum and Angela had shared.

"Don't say things like that, Davey," she said, hating her slightly sycophantic tone. But she hated it when he was in a bad mood. His smile lit her up but when he was down, it was like a black cloud hanging over the day. She couldn't bear it.

"I suppose I can tell Maudie I'm busy," she said doubtfully.

"That's my girl," he said, rewarding her with another kiss.

On Saturday evening, Davey called for Elise, and they walked together to the hall. Maudie and Fred were already there. Maudie came over, and kissed Elise on the cheek. "Guess what, Maudie? Fred says he wants to marry me. When he's saved enough money, for a place of our own."

Davey, overhearing, snorted. "Sometime next century, then."

Maudie glared at him and Elise squeezed her hand. "Well, I think that's lovely."

"Got you a ring, has he?" Davey peered over, as if examining Maudie's hand.

"No, not yet. I told him a ring doesn't matter, anyway."

"Of course it doesn't," Elise took her friend's arm and led her away from Davey, whose mood swings were so unpredictable. He'd been full of fun on the way here, and now he had that look about him. The mean one. She didn't want him pouring cold water on Maudie's happiness.

She let her friend tell her all the details of the conversation she'd had with Fred, and how many children they both wanted, and the names they liked, but all the while she was uncomfortably aware of Davey looking disapprovingly across. For a while, Fred had tried to engage him in pleasant conversation, but she could see that hadn't worked. Lovely Fred. Smiling and kind, she was sure now that Maudie had been telling the truth about that night when the two of them had disappeared. Surely he was not the type of boy to take Maudie down a side alley and do god-knew-what to her; and she was ashamed she had thought Maudie was the type of girl who would let him.

After a while, Fred came to take Maudie's hand and whisk her onto the floor for a dance. Elise made her way back to Davey.

"Come on, we're going," he said, his brow heavy and knotted.

"Now? We haven't even had a dance."

"Not tonight, Elise," he said, pulling her roughly.

"Ow, that hurts."

"Don't be a baby."

He stalked out and she followed him, keen to put right whatever was wrong.

"Shall we go down to the beach?" she suggested, thinking how much she had loved it there that night she had gone for a walk in the darkness. Maybe the peace and solitude would soothe Davey's troubles away.

"Are you mad? It's the middle of the night." But he

stopped and looked at her, and she thought his expression softened. "Is that what you want?" he asked.

"I… yes, I think it would be nice."

"Alright, then."

They walked in silence, but it didn't feel as heavy as it had. Davey's steps seemed lighter, somehow, and his pace picked up. When they got to the top of the slope to the sand, he pushed her playfully. "Race you down!"

She looked at him, relief flooding through her, that the prospect of the beach had lightened his mood. And it had been her idea, she congratulated herself. Maudie might think he was a bad choice, but Elise knew Davey was a good person, really. He just needed somebody who understood him.

"Just a sec," she stooped, as if to adjust her shoe, then she began to run.

"Hey! You cheat," he shouted after her, but he caught her easily and as they reached the sand, his hand grabbed at her arm and he yanked her back. It hurt and, before she knew it, he had pulled her down onto the cold, damp beach. His fingers were tight on her arm, and she had a flashback to Lord Camelford-Bassett. She put her other hand on Davey's, gently trying to ease his fingers a little, without him noticing. It only made him grip her tighter, and his other hand found its way to her opposite arm. He pushed on her so that she was lying on the cold beach and he above her, his weight moving onto her.

"Davey?" she said. "What are you doing?"

"You know full well what I'm doing," he said.

"No, no, Davey, I'm not…"

His mouth silenced her, rough and hard. He kissed her in a way he had not before, and she fought for her breath, not sure whether it was the strength of his mouth, or the shock of his actions.

She tried to wriggle free. He pulled back, but kept hold of her arms.

"Come on, Elise. I know all about you and his lordship at the manor. Don't think we don't all know why they let you go."

"What?" She felt like she'd been slapped in the face. She had pushed all thoughts of her time at Tregynon from her mind. The kiss with Lord Camelford-Bassett had been a huge mistake, which he had instigated. She felt sure he must have regretted it and put it all behind him as well.

"Don't think you were the first," he laughed. "You did think that, didn't you? Did you think you were special? You're lucky I want you, after what you did with him."

His mouth was on hers again, and this time she didn't struggle. Was this it, then? Was this the way the world worked? She wished somebody had told her.

He eased his hand inside her dress, and she let him. He pulled at her clothes, and told her he loved her, and she let it all happen, hoping it would make him smile again.

Elise

I haven't yet had a chance to tell Louisa about Davey. Well, that's not quite true. I haven't really wanted to. We've been having such a nice time, it seems a shame to ruin it. And I can't do it tonight, because tonight we will be dining with AJ. I am quite excited about this. It's almost as if I'm going on a date myself. I've found myself wondering what to wear, thinking about putting a bit of make-up on. I don't want Louisa to feel ashamed of me, or embarrassed by her old Cornish mum. Though I'm more London than she is, if truth be told. London, born and bred – for the first few years of my life, at any rate.

The plan is that I will walk up to the hotel late this afternoon, to meet Louisa and AJ for pre-dinner drinks.

I have been very good and stopped myself from making flippant comments about how posh this sounds. I don't want Louisa getting annoyed with me, or impatient. And I will pretend that I always have pre-dinner drinks at posh hotels (well, the poshest this town has to offer, at any rate), even though neither of us really believes that.

I'm looking forward to seeing the old place again, as well. Tregynon Hotel. Tregynon Manor, as was, and for a few years the Whiteley School for Girls. I have been up there a few times over the years and, just like Lanhydrock, it has changed, and yet it hasn't. When the company bought it twenty years ago, from Charles

Camelford-Bassett – who I would have dearly loved to see but I don't suppose would remember me – they 'retained much of the original charm', according to their literature. And from what I can see, this is true. Except they have added a swimming pool and spa, which I bet her ladyship would have loved, and tennis courts, too.

Louisa has caved in and admitted to me that she has work to do that cannot wait, so that is what she has been doing this afternoon: "But I really don't mind, Mum. I might just stay in and get through some of it today, if you don't mind. Then I won't have to think about it and I can relax this evening."

"Of course I don't mind, love." And I don't; not really. I wonder if she's also nervous about AJ's imminent arrival – and if she too is wondering what to wear.

As it happens, it's a Caring the Community day anyway, so I've been up there this morning. As ever, talk is of the Saltings and developments there.

"Blocking the view with their posh new houses."

"Well, they may not go to holiday-makers," I said.

"Rubbish! You know as well as I do, Elise, there's none round here that can afford that sort of money. They can barely afford them so-called affordable houses that's being built."

"True enough," I said. "But you know, it's happening. There's not a lot we can do about it, so we might as well try and look on the bright side."

Bill shot me a questioning look. I've generally been quite quiet about the whole thing, preferring to let people's protests and complaints go over my head. Now, though, I feel like I have a vested interest... what with AJ's links to Canyon Holdings, and his link to Louisa, and my link to her... it's tenuous, of course, but it's making me feel a bit different about the whole thing.

"What do you think, Maggie?" Bill asked as she passed.

I smiled at my new friend. We don't really make a thing of knowing each other when we're at the club. I don't really know why not. It just feels right, not to broadcast our growing friendship.

"About what?" she stopped and smiled around the group.

"The changing face of the town," he said sarcastically.

"Ah, the Saltings?" she asked. "Well, you have to remember it's been on the go longer than I've lived here, so I don't really know what the place was like before it. I can understand why it's got people's backs up. And I can also see it might be quite an exciting prospect for the youngsters. Things to do... and even jobs for some of them, I'd think."

"You seen how much a film ticket is?" Jim scoffed. "Think many of our youngsters can afford those kinds of prices?"

"I'd heard that they're planning to make some local concessions," she said. "Membership cards, discounts, that kind of thing."

"Sounds reasonable," I said, and Bill gave me another funny look.

"About as reasonable as them bricking over the fisherman's yard."

"Ah, but they're giving them more space, aren't they? And putting up a building for them," Maggie said, and I looked at her, surprised. I had no idea she knew so much about it all, or had that much interest, for that matter.

"Are they?" Bill asked, equally surprised.

"Yes, John Price lives next door to me, he said they've just agreed it. They're pretty happy with the idea, I think." I noticed Maggie's cheeks were flushing.

"Who are? The Canyon people?"

"No, the fishermen. The fleet."

"Nothing to say they won't take it away again," Jim was determined to find the downside. "Private harbour, see? Belongs to those boys in London."

And girls, I thought but still said nothing.

"Well, yes, I suppose. I don't know. I'm just passing on what I've heard."

"Well, good for you, girl. You've not been here a year, and you know more than us old timers," Bill said kindly.

"It's not what you know, it's who you know," I said, and thought Maggie looked uncomfortable. Maybe she felt like she'd said too much, or sounded too positive. "Anyway," I said, in a clumsy bid to change the subject, "have I told you I'm dining out tonight?"

"With your Louisa?" Bill asked approvingly. He'd given Lou her very first job, doing the filing and packing for his seed-packet business.

"Yes. And her new man." I couldn't help myself, even though I know better than to feed the gossip. Not that Bill and Jim are particularly inclined to that sort of thing.

"That right?" asked Bill. "About time she settled down." He cast a laughing glance my way, knowing full well my reaction to that kind of comment.

"I'll send her along to give you a piece of her mind if you're not careful," I said. "You wouldn't like that."

"No, don't suppose I would."

"That's exciting," Maggie smiled. "I look forward to hearing all about it... next week," she added. "Now, I'd better get this lot in the kitchen and washed up." Laden down with a tray of cups and saucers, she headed away.

"You must be pleased, Elise," said Bill.

"I'll reserve judgement till I've met him," I said. "But he sounds nice, and she seems happy. What more could I want than that?"

At four o'clock, just as I'm self-consciously rubbing off the little bit of blusher that I'd brushed across my cheeks, my phone starts ringing. I go downstairs, only for it to ring off just as I get to it. Then I hear my mobile vibrating, only it's upstairs.

"Bugger it," I mutter to myself, and gamely go up the stairs again, only thinking halfway up that I should have brought the other phone with me, just in case the mobile rings off and they try the normal phone again. Luckily, this doesn't happen, although I don't get to my mobile in time. I pick it up and see Louisa's name on the screen. I call her back.

"He isn't coming, Mum," she says, sounding very much like she's trying to sound as though she isn't bothered either way.

"Oh, love," I say, unable to keep the sympathy from my voice. It feels like the time she was stood up by Bobby Carver.

"It's fine," she says tightly. "Just one of those things."

"But everything's... alright... between you?" I'm trying to tiptoe carefully here. I have loved being in her confidence these last few days. If I put a foot wrong now, though, I risk blowing it.

"It's fine," she snaps, but is immediately contrite. "Sorry, Mum, yes everything's fine. But I think maybe...

maybe I've been a bit too keen with him. He said he had to stay in London, but I could tell something wasn't right." I hold my breath, sorry for her, but unable to stop myself feeling pleased that she is talking to me. Confiding in me still. "I asked him, outright. Did he actually want to come down in the first place?"

That's my girl. Never less than direct. Though maybe it doesn't do her any favours, in these kinds of situations. "And what did he say?"

"He said yes, and then he said no. Well, he dithered, which was annoying, to be honest. I don't have time for ditherers. Said he felt like it was a bit much, too soon. Coming down to Cornwall, coming out for a meal with you. Even though I tried to tell him what you're like. That it wouldn't be some kind of formal, meet-the-parents thing. Just that I think you two would like each other."

"Really?" I can't help but feel pleased, and try not to sound it.

"Yes, really, Mum." She sighs, but fondly. "I know I'm not very good at showing it but I'm proud of you, and I wanted him to meet you and see, see where I'm from. I mean, he's involved in the Saltings, and he's going to be managing community engagement–" I'm glad she couldn't see me roll my eyes at this "– and I thought it would be good for him to meet you from that perspective, too. Somebody who's lived here nearly all their life but has a good, balanced view of things. Not hysterical, like lots of folk round here."

Her use of the word 'folk' also makes me smile. Makes her sound like her roots are here – which of course they are.

"Well, thank you, Louisa, for saying that. I really do appreciate it. But I'm so sorry he's not coming. I was looking forward to meeting him. I even had some blusher on."

This at least makes her laugh.

"Yeah, well, maybe it will happen another time. I don't know, though, Mum. I feel like it's gone off the boil. You know when you just know? I think I've been kidding myself. Making it seem like it was meant to be – what with his links to this place. And the fact that he's not a dick – sorry – at work, to me or any of the other women, or lesser mortals. He's always friendly to the doorman, the cleaners, the guys that deliver the bottles of water... and he's pretty good-looking too, which always helps."

"Maybe it's not dead in the water yet, love."

"Maybe. But I think I know. If I'm honest, I pushed it, this trip down here, and him coming down this week. I should have read the signs, but I ignored them. I think I just wanted this to happen. Maybe I'm going soft in my old age. But I think I'd like a relationship. A proper relationship."

I'm sorry for her, and I share her disappointment. It's been nice seeing her enthusiastic about AJ, and to see her priorities shifting a bit."

"I suppose, if it's made you realise that, then maybe it's not been a waste altogether. Perhaps he's not the right one for you but if you want a 'right one' I'm sure he's out there. Perhaps AJ's just the catalyst for you keeping an eye out."

"Maybe," she laughs. "He's too young for me anyway!"

"Rubbish," I laugh. "If men can do it, women can too. Anyway, we can still have our dinner, can't we? And pre-dinner drinks," I say.

"We can. Of course we can. I'd like that, Mum."

1951

The wedding was inevitable, and nobody was happy about it, even though Elise tried to convince herself that she at least was. And Davey. He loved her, didn't he? He said so often enough. Angela, though, and Maudie, and Davey's family, who she had met only a handful of times, were dead-set against it. Fred – wonderfully kind and gentle Fred – would not be drawn either way.

"It's Elise's choice, isn't it? Hers and Davey's. And if they're happy, then we must be happy for them."

"The problem is, I don't think they are happy," Maudie replied. "And the wedding they're having – all for show, it seems to me. It'll be his dad, putting the pressure on, wanting things to look all right and proper. They've got the mayor coming, and some of the chamber of commerce. Elise doesn't know them, and isn't happy about them being there, but she hasn't much of a leg to stand on. It's a chance for him to show off his wealth, though he's no better than you and I."

Fred and Maudie had their own wedding coming up, which was to be a far simpler affair than their friends'. A simple church wedding, with family and a few friends, followed by drinks and sandwiches at the village hall; with the promise of some dancing to music provided by Fred's uncle and his accordion.

It was three weeks after Davey's and Elise's wedding, even though Maudie and Fred had been engaged first, and set the date of their own special day.

"It's like one-upmanship on his part," Fred had huffed, in a rare moment of ill temper.

"It's not *like it*. It *is it*," Maudie said, cuddling in closer to Fred on the sofa in her front room. Her mum allowed her and Fred some occasional time in there, to get away from her mischievous brothers. It felt good to be united in disapproval, but she was uneasy at the thought of Elise marrying Davey. She knew what he could be like, but she had tried to warn her friend, and now, with a baby on the way, there really was no choice.

Angela wanted to be the one to give Elise away. "I'm the closest thing you have to a parent," she said, "and you're the closest I have to a child."

The Plummers would not hear of it, though. There was a heated exchange between Angela and Mr Plummer, while Mrs Plummer sat timidly, either not wishing, or too scared, to be involved.

Elise's dress was bought by the Plummers – a second- or possibly even third-hand gown cleverly doctored by Maudie. "This is my wedding present to you," Maudie said to Elise. She'd begun to get some work around town, as a seamstress, which she did in the evenings while Fred sat by, reading or chatting with her brothers. Once he and Maudie were married, they would be living together at her family home; her parents had cleared out the attic room, which was pokey and cold in the winter, but unbearably hot in the summer. Still, it was their own space, until they could afford a place of their own. Anything extra she earned from her sewing would go towards that, and she was fast forgetting the idea of progressing her law career.

There were tears in her eyes – and Angela's – when they looked at Elise. The bump was barely beginning to show, on Elise's slight frame, and was entirely obscured by the panel which Maudie had sewn into the dress.

"You look beautiful," Maudie said. "Davey'd better appreciate it."

"He better had," Angela agreed. "I'm going to miss having you here, Elise."

"I'll miss you, too."

"Can't believe you're going to be up there on that cliff," Maudie said. "If it gets too lonely, you come down any time, you hear?"

"Yes, there's always a room for you here, Elise. You know that, don't you?"

"I won't be too far away," said Elise, "but I won't be able to come and stay, you know. Not once I'm married. I'll have my own house to keep."

Davey's family had gifted a small house, which had belonged to an elderly aunt, to their son and his wife-to-be, in a hamlet a mile or two out of town, on a windswept clifftop with far-reaching views across the sea to the front, and the moors behind.

Angela and Maudie looked at each other but said nothing. They knew they were defeated. Once Elise was married, she was no longer theirs, and no longer her own woman. She would be Davey's, and it was very clear that was how he saw things.

The day itself was as bright and blue-skied as it was possible to be. Even though the year was creeping onwards into autumn, the air was warm, and the trees still in full leaf. Elise looked out of her bedroom window, listening to the garden birds, and the sea, and felt her heart soar. She was to be married, and she was to be a mother. Which one of those things was more exciting, she wasn't sure. She just hoped that in marrying Davey, he would finally believe that she loved him and would stay true to him. As if there was any doubt about that.

She fervently wished that she had never encountered Lord Camelford-Bassett, much less kissed him, but she also believed that life had to take its own path. And had that not happened, she may not have gone to work at Fawcett's, or met Maudie, or Davey.

Mr Fawcett had been very sorry to see her go but once she became engaged, his attitude towards her had changed; he became more distant, and apparently more respectful, although it is possible it was Davey's right to Elise that he was swayed by, rather than any change in attitude towards Elise herself. Equally likely, in such a small town, he may have known about, or at least guessed at, her pregnancy. Mr Fawcett had been interviewing new 'girls' – just slightly younger than Elise and Maudie, but they seemed like young foals to Elise; just learning to stand on their own feet. She wished them well and hoped that they would learn to handle Mr Fawcett and his lewd comments and wandering eyes.

Elise and Angela were driven to the church by one of Davey's uncles. There were two bridesmaids – daughters of said uncle – and it was down to him to give her away.

"You were never his to begin with. You were never anyone's but your own. You remember that, Elise. No matter what." Angela had been slightly mollified that she did at least get to travel with Elise. "You be happy, my girl, as happy as can be. I know what a wonderful mother you'll be," she whispered. "But if you ever need anything, you know where I am."

"I do," Elise squeezed her hand. "Thank you, Miss Forbes," she smiled.

"Miss Forbes!" Angela laughed. "Don't give me that!"

The small church was full and the organ was playing as Elise walked up the aisle towards Davey. The vicar was smiling, too, and the service had Elise in tears. She could hardly believe that this was all happening to her. It almost felt as if she were looking in on someone else's life.

Afterwards, she and Davey were driven in the same car to the Peal o'Bells, at the top of the town. There was bunting waving in the wind and children playing in the field out back. Drinks were had; beer for Davey, and an orange juice for Elise. It was a rare treat, and she savoured the slightly acidic sweetness, hoping it wouldn't bring on the heartburn she'd started to expect.

Davey talked and laughed with the men, whilst Elise sat with Maudie and Angela, and Davey's mum, watching the children playing in the field behind. There was a pony in the next field and Elise imagined her own little boy or girl with a pony of their own. Who knew what life might bring?

Over time, people began to filter away and it was soon time for her and Davey to be taken off to their new home. She had barely seen him since they'd been at the pub, and was dismayed to see that he was quite drunk. It was his wedding day, though, she reasoned.

She waved and smiled bravely at Angela and Maudie, who were gathered with the other remaining guests to see them off.

Davey, sitting in the front with his uncle, looked back at her and smiled. "You look nice, Elise."

Nice, she thought. Just *nice*. He looked as handsome as anything in a suit, with his sun-kissed skin and his hair lightened from a long, hot summer.

She wanted to kiss him, she realised, and felt elated that now she really was allowed to. They could do anything they wanted, and nobody could disapprove. It would soon become obvious, that she was pregnant, and if the baby came a bit early, who would say anything? Now it was all above board. They were married.

The cottage door was open when they arrived, and somebody had pinned a bunch of flowers to it.

"How lovely!" Elise marvelled, stopping to smell them.

Davey wandered in, and parked himself on one of the chairs. "Shut the door and come here," he smiled at her.

She did as she was bid, and he pulled her onto his knee. He put his arms around her and kissed her, his breath hot and beery. She wanted to change out of her wedding dress, feeling like his hands would tarnish it. She loved that dress, and wanted to keep it forever. But she dared not say anything to Davey and instead let him kiss her, and put his hands all over her. He stood, suddenly, and unsteadily; easily lifting her, though, and carrying her up the stairs to their bedroom.

"Mrs Plummer," he said, placing her on the bed and moving on top of her.

The baby, she wanted to say. *Mind the baby*. But she couldn't, and wouldn't. She was his now. They were married.

Afterwards, they lay in bed, and Davey was soon snoring. She turned her head to the window, to see clouds scudding into view. The daylight was becoming dimmer, and it looked like there was rain far out to sea. She pulled herself up for a better look, pulling the covers up as well, though nobody could see her.

It felt strange to be in bed on an afternoon. It was a Saturday, and she pictured the bustle down in town, feeling a little lurch of homesickness. Funny, when it had taken her so long to feel at home there. Still, she had this view now, she thought, and she sat for some time just watching the ever-changing scene, with the shifting shapes of clouds and shades of grey and brown and gold across the water; the sun breaking through every now and then but vanquished each time.

She looked at Davey. Her husband. His mouth was slightly open, and he was snoring gently. "Davey," she whispered, but to no avail. She decided to explore. In the next room – a tiny bedroom fit for a nursery – was her bag of clothes, which she could now unpack. She selected a pair of trousers and a jumper, as it felt colder now than it had this morning, and got dressed. She tiptoed back into the main bedroom and rescued her wedding dress, which Davey had pulled from her. *Careful*, she had wanted to say, but she hadn't. She was relieved now to see it was all still as it had been. Hanging it in the doorway, she went downstairs, where it really did feel cold. The grate had been already set for a fire, she was not sure by whom, so she set about lighting it, and filling the kettle. She thought of the electric kettle at Fawcett's and wondered if she and Davey might have one of them one day.

While the water was heating, she went outside. The cottage was at one end of a terrace of three, but there was no sign of their neighbours. To the side and rear was a garden, which had already been put to use for vegetables, originally for the war effort. The soil had been cleared and turned and Elise picked up a handful, letting it drop through her fingers. She smelled her hand, inhaling the scent of earth. She might miss the busyness of town, but she was overjoyed to have a garden of her own, to do with as she pleased. Davey had already made it clear that he had no interest in it.

Elise stood strong and straight, and turned slowly, 360 degrees. This was her home, now, and this was the first day of the rest of her life.

Back inside, the kettle was whistling. She made tea for two and carried a tray carefully up to the bedroom, placing it on the dresser.

"Davey," she said, "I made us some tea."

He grunted, and groaned. "My head."

"Are you alright?" Elise asked but he pushed past her, and went downstairs. Into the bathroom, which had been built as an add-on to the old cottage. Elise followed him down and could hear what sounded like him being sick.

"Are you alright?" she asked again.

"Do I sound alright?" came the reply.

She didn't know what to do. Should she wait outside for him? Or go and have her cup of tea, which she was really desperate for, having had nothing to drink but that orange juice.

She opted for the latter, and went back upstairs, listening nervously for signs of movement below. When she heard him emerge from the bathroom, she scurried back down the stairs, and hovered in the hall doorway.

"I feel like shit," he said. He looked like it, too. She

pushed back the thought.

"Come and have your cup of tea," she said. "It might help."

"I'm going back to the Peal."

"The pub?"

"Yeah. They're open again in half an hour."

"But you've just been…"

"What?" His eyes flashed dark and angry. "I'm fine. It's my wedding day, I deserve to celebrate, don't I? There's a few boys who haven't bought me a drink yet."

He pushed past her and out into the late afternoon, the day now thoroughly grey and gloomy as it waited for nightfall to put it out of its misery.

Elise shut the door and pulled nervously at her sleeves. *Pull yourself together.* She decided to set about making this quiet, empty house a home.

The signs were all there, but she didn't want to see them. Not yet.

Elise

I meet Louisa as arranged, in the hotel bar. Which was once the library. Hard to believe it's the same room where I used to have French lessons, and geography, and then later where I taught little Tabitha, Edmond and Charles. If I let myself, I can still see him now, Lord Camelford-Bassett, swanning in and making his presence known.

My daughter is sitting at the bar itself, on one of those high stools. Small and neat, with glossy black hair, from behind it would be hard to guess her age. When she turns, her years are more apparent, but in a sophisticated way; such that I could never achieve, with my frizzy hair and ruddy cheeks.

"Mum," she smiles and raises her glass. In fact, it's my glass, as it turns out. A martini, with an olive on a stick. My daughter has the good sense to realise that the bar stools are not for me, and so she comes to greet me, smiling warmly as she kisses my cheek and suggesting we take one of the tables by the window.

I am very happy to. Bright sunshine is bathing the patio outside, where tables have been strategically placed. Beyond is the lawn, where the boys once ran, arms outstretched like fighter plane wings. Further still, the little beach, which the hotel mentions proudly on its website. *Take an evening stroll to our own private beach, and watch the proud fishing fleet return to harbour.*

"How are you, my love?" I ask Lou, as we take our seats.

"I'm fine, Mum," she says. "Honestly."

I'm glad she isn't feeling spikey, or defensive. It must mean she's not too devastated by developments with her American.

"I'm glad." I raise my glass to hers and then take a sip. It is delicious, but tastes strong. "I'd better make this last," I say. "I'm not used to cocktails. Just the odd small glass of wine, or cider."

"Well, I wanted to treat you, Mum. And to the meal tonight."

"Thank you, that's lovely of you."

We sit companionably for a while. I take it all in. The room has high ceilings and feels so clean and fresh, with white walls and tasteful artwork from local artists and photographers, where there used to be dark, imposing shelves full of books. As I sip my drink, I realise I am drinking far too quickly, and I'm certainly feeling it. But it's a nice feeling, sitting here with my daughter. And I know now, I need to tell her, what she needs to know. Whether AJ is egging her on or not.

"Lou," I say, and she looks at me, her cheeks appealingly flushed. "You asked, you know, about your dad."

"Yes," she says, "I did."

"Do you still want to know? What he was like?"

"Yes, I do."

"Well, OK, then. I'm going to tell you. And I wonder if you already know some of this…" At that moment, a waitress – Hetty Jakins' granddaughter, if I'm not mistaken – appears at my side. "Your table's ready," she says.

"I'll tell you in a minute," I say, in a stage whisper, as I stand and really feel that alcohol kick in.

"OK." Louisa smiles and takes my arm. We walk together behind the waitress. "But you don't have to, Mum. Not if you don't want to."

So she does know something, or has guessed something. "No. It's fine. I want to. I suppose it needs telling, before I…"

"Don't, Mum," Louisa looks quickly at me, her eyes shining. "Don't say it."

"Alright, love. Alright." I'm slightly stunned by her strength of feeling.

We take our seats in the dining room (which was always the dining room when the school was here, and when the Camelford-Bassetts reclaimed their home – not that I was ever invited to dine with them, of course), thanking the waitress, and picking up our menus. "Let's order first, Mum. Then we can talk. If you want to."

I do as I'm told, and order the sea bream, with new potatoes and spinach. Louisa asks if I'd like a starter, but I know my limits these days. No doubt a starter would make a perfectly fine main course for me, but I'm not going to say that.

When our orders are taken and Louisa has selected some white wine, which has been brought to our table and she's tasted and proclaimed delicious, we are left to our own devices, and so I begin again.

"Alright, Louisa. Back to your dad. Davey." My mind travels back across the dividing line between the centuries, flying over the years like a crow crossing farmland. "He was a good-looking man. Best-looking boy in town, they used to say, and they were right."

Louisa smiles slightly unsurely – hearing the words but detecting my tone.

"We met when I was at work, with Maudie, at Fawcett's. When everybody left from the school, well except for Angela, I stayed on here. You know I worked up here as a governess, at first, but then I came back to town and met Maudie, and I met Davey. Who was Maudie's boyfriend at the time."

"He wasn't!" Louisa's eyes are shining at this juicy piece of gossip.

"He was. But not for long. And she was soon with Fred, which was the right choice for her. Davey asked me out, and I said yes. A bad move in a little town like this and I wasn't very popular for a while, I can tell you. Some upstart from the private girls' school, coming and stealing one of their men. Of course, it wasn't like that. I wasn't an upstart, and I wasn't stealing anybody. If anyone was stealing something, it was Davey."

"What do you mean, Mum? What did he steal?"

"Do you mean…? No, it wasn't like that. Not really." I think of the night on the beach. Consent is what they talk about these days, isn't it? I didn't not consent, but when I look back I think it was obvious it wasn't really what I wanted. But that's water under the bridge now. And not something I particularly want to dwell on.

"I suppose I mean it in a less literal sense. At first, he was everything I thought I wanted. A boy, my age, good-looking and popular, or so I thought. And he had a well-paying job at his family's business. He wasn't always very happy, and I thought I could change that. I wanted to, to make him happy. Sometimes, he was lovely. But, he liked a drink," I say, looking at my own half-empty

glass. Or should that be half-full? "And he had a temper."
I look at her.

"Oh. Oh, Mum," she says.

"It wasn't that he was always nasty; not at first. But he did like to tell me what to do. And you know me. I don't really like being told what to do."

Louisa smiles knowingly at this, knowing also that she is just the same.

"Back then, though, I let it all happen to me. It felt like everything was always decided for me. Even going to Whiteley; that was Mum's choice, not mine, though I know why she did it. Moving to Cornwall – decided by the school and maybe local government, I don't really know. After school, Angela found me the job here and said I could live with her. It was incredibly kind of her but again, I had no real option. It's like I was on a conveyor belt, just being carried along through my own life. Then I was with Davey – which ironically was about the only choice I'd really made myself – and ended up pregnant, with Laurie – who else? And then we were married, but by then I don't think we liked each other much at all."

"I'm so sorry, Mum. I didn't realise it happened like that. Although, I shouldn't be surprised," she exclaims, all fiery. "And I suppose you couldn't go it alone. Not then."

"Not then, indeed," I say, "and if I'm honest, I wouldn't have wanted to. I wouldn't have known where to start. I couldn't even remember my own dad, but he had died, so Mum was a respectable widow. I couldn't be a single mother, it was viewed very differently then. I was stuck. Trapped, really. But I never for one minute resented being pregnant. That only ever seemed a good thing."

"And Dad…?"

"He was reliable, in that he brought home the money. I was never sure how much, because a lot of it also went on drink, but there was still more than enough left over. And of course, we had the house, from his family, and we didn't have to worry about rent, or a mortgage."

"Was he pleased you were pregnant?"

"I suppose he was, in his way. But he wasn't very interested. He was glad Laurie was a boy, I remember that."

Her face falls. "So, when I was born…?"

"When you were born, Louisa, and he held you, he was like a different person. I don't think I'd ever seen so much love on his face."

She is appeased by this, but it really is true. I remember his face, gazing down at his daughter. And, naïve girl that I was, I thought perhaps that she might be the thing that changed him. Finally made him the man that I wanted him to be.

"My girl," he had said. "My little girl." And he'd sworn to be better, do better, back then, and for a while he did. But do I tell her that? I don't. She has been disappointed enough for one day.

"But he was an unhappy man, Louisa, and there was nothing any of us could have done to change that. I think his dad was unhappy before him, and I know he could be very hard on Davey. Seems like that got passed on, and I was on the receiving end. But you need to know that no matter how he behaved to me, he never did anything like that to you or Laurie."

Again, this is true, or almost. I had felt Davey's burgeoning irritation with Laurie, as my little boy got bigger, and feared for how things might go when he grew older. As things happened, I never found out.

"Did he... hit you, Mum?" Louisa asks now, in a hushed tone, across the table. I look out of the window to see a boat coming in, heading to the harbour. The first of the fleet to return tonight.

The waitress chooses this moment to deliver our plates and so I wait, and thank her, and so does Louisa. We look at our food.

"He did, my girl, I'm sorry to say."

"Once... or more than once?"

"More often than I can remember."

"When we were there?"

"Sometimes."

"I don't remember."

"I'm glad. Does Laurie?"

"I... don't know. I've never asked him."

"But he doesn't like to talk about his dad?"

"No."

Tears are glistening in Louisa's eyes, and I know they are reflected in my own.

"Louisa," I say, "you can ask me any questions you like. And it doesn't have to be tonight. If you want to talk more, we can, but we could also just enjoy our meal, if you'd prefer. I am not intending to shuffle off this mortal coil any time soon, and I promise I'll answer your questions honestly."

"OK, Mum." She thinks for a moment. "I do want to ask this, and then maybe you're right, we should try to just enjoy our meal, and being together. But it's a hard question to ask."

I already know what it is. "You want to know if your

dad killed himself?"

"Yes," she looks down, then back up at me. "I do."

"I can promise you, my beautiful girl, that he didn't. That is one thing of which I can be sure."

She looks relieved. "Really?"

"Really."

"I did have one more thing," she says now, twisting her napkin in her hands.

"Ask away."

"Can I come home with you tonight? Stay with you, till I go back to London?"

"Louisa," I gasp, struck nearly breathless with surprise. "You can come back home any time you like. Any time."

We smile at each other, and laugh at our shared tears. Then we tuck into our food, hungry and relieved and, for my part at least, brimming with an unexpected joy.

1951

When Laurie was born, Davey was nowhere to be seen. Their neighbour, Marie, who Elise had grown quite close to, was on hand instead. She had four children of her own and she sent the oldest, Daniel, running to town, to see if he could locate Davey. In the meantime, Elise sweated and panted, and cried out in agony, and eventually cried out again, but a little more quietly, when her baby boy was placed in her arms. Small and loud, and shiny and new, she held him close and whispered into the top of his head. Her husband was nowhere to be seen, and she was glad.

Davey showed next to no interest in the baby Laurie, but as the boy grew a little bit older and a little bit more interesting, his attitude began to change.

Everybody, and particularly Davey's own mother, remarked at how similar the boy was to his dad, and Davey seemed to like this. "You'll follow in my footsteps, eh, won't you lad?" Elise hoped not.

She was glad that her husband was absent much of the time. His own father's health was failing, and Davey had stepped into his shoes in the business. It was hard work, as he wasn't shy of telling her, and all he wanted at the end of the day was his tea, and not to be bothered.

You forgot to mention the drink, Elise thought, but she dared not say anything.

Though she loved her baby with all her heart, she often looked wistfully back to the days at Fawcett's, when she and Maudie would chat and laugh and gossip in the office. Those snatched moments at lunchtime in the sunshine, or even in the rain, sheltering under the tree in the graveyard. It all seemed like the ultimate freedom these days. School was a distant memory, and she had long since lost touch with Violet, who would still be at university. Would Violet be disappointed in her schoolfriend, whose life had turned to housework and motherhood?

Maudie, meanwhile, was still very much around, but could only visit Elise illicitly, dodging Davey's disapproval. She loved little Laurie and often talked about becoming pregnant, with sadness. She and Fred had been trying for some time, but something wasn't working. On the plus side, her business was going from strength to strength, while Fred had found surprising success as a door-to-door vacuum cleaner salesman. Their fortunes were improving, and Maudie said proudly that they were buying a place of their own.

"In town?" Elise asked, not wanting to think that her friend might move away.

"Oh yes, of course. One of the new places. Near our families. And friends," Maudie said.

She was concerned for Elise, but it was a very difficult subject to broach. Her friend was loyal, and prickly if she felt that Davey was being criticised, but Maudie could see that since having Laurie she had lost a lot of weight, so that she was thinner than she had been before. She also seemed more subdued.

Maudie, too, often looked back on those Fawcett's days with fondness. Before life became about weddings, and babies – or wanting babies, at least – and mortgages. There was a lot to be said for having a little more money, and Fred was a good'un, that was for sure. He would never tell her what to do, and he was a kind, gentle and fun man, who her family loved. And he supported her business venture, and long hours (which sometimes meant she was not always able to cook their tea, but he'd just cook instead). As time went on, and their longed-for pregnancy failed to materialise, Fred became stronger and more protective. It would have annoyed Maudie before, but now she was grateful for his sensitivity. She knew she could look after herself, but sometimes it felt good to have somebody to look after her. He told her he loved her, and always would, and that they would find a way to have children. Adoption, if necessary. "There are a lot of kids out there who need homes, Maud. Who might need us," he said.

She had cried in his arms and let the deep, heartfelt grief out. It felt good to be so open and honest with him and it was that moment, really, which cemented their relationship. She looked back on those days when she'd been with Davey, and shuddered to think it might have been him who she had ended up with. Maybe, just maybe, she'd have had her longed-for baby with him, but was a lifetime with him really a price worth paying?

***

There came a time when Davey's father died and it seemed to hit him hard, despite his contempt for his dad, who had become a weak old man while Davey grew in stature and strength. Laurie, by now five years old, was almost mute at home when his dad was about, although he could be loving and chatty when it was just him and his mum. Angela, now the headmistress of the small school, said he was bright and forthcoming in class. Elise was glad. It was just his dad's overbearing presence that had him tongue-tied.

"You stupid little…!" At the cottage on the cliff, Davey shouted at Laurie, who looked from his dad to his mum, lip trembling and eyes full of fear. It was a Sunday afternoon and the little boy, who had been playing with his train track, had jumped up with excitement at something, knocking over his dad's beer.

Davey, who had been just about fit to doze off, his stomach full from the Sunday roast he insisted on Elise making, was instantly enraged. "Look what you're doing, you little idiot!"

Laurie went running into his mum's arms.

"You're making a sissy of him," Davey hissed. "Little mummy's boy, aren't you?"

"You're alright," Elise said to Laurie, throwing a look at Davey. She might be subdued, as Maudie had observed, but her spirit was not altogether rubbed out, and especially not when it came to her son.

"Don't you look at me like that, woman," Davey grumbled, and stood up, leaving his glass on the floor, its spilled contents creeping through the cracks in the floorboards. He grabbed his coat and cap from the hook, and left, without a backward glance.

Elise, shaking with fear or anger, or possibly both, held Laurie to her. Later, she took him into the garden and they dug for potatoes, then she fed and bathed him and put him to bed long before his father returned. She knew that Laurie was as glad not to see Davey as she was and she went to bed early herself, so she could pretend to be asleep when her husband returned home.

The first time Davey hit her had been long before, when she was pregnant, but he had seemed truly contrite.

"I'm so sorry," he had said – sobbed, almost. "I promised myself I wouldn't do that. I wouldn't be like him."

Elise, who found it hard to see anybody upset, had held him, as though he were a child, and told him it was alright. That first time, she remembered. It had shocked her beyond words. They'd been sitting down to tea, and she'd forgotten to get the salt and pepper. She had stood to get them and he'd sprung up, blocking her way. "I work my arse off, woman, all day long, and what do you do?"

Elise's hands had gone protectively to her stomach.

"That's all you care about now, isn't it? You don't care about me at all."

It didn't make any sense, but Davey's rages rarely did. She knew better than to question him, though. She looked him in the eye, determined not to let him see her fear, and went to move past him. *Whack.* The back of his hand cracked across her right cheek. She stumbled against the wall, stunned and unsure for a moment as to what had just happened. Slowly, she brought her own hand to her face, and looked back at her husband in disbelief. His face fell, and he moved towards her. She had her back against the wall, and nowhere to go. She was terrified. But he put his hands on her arms, moved them up to her jaw. "I'm sorry, I'm so sorry," he said. "Please believe me. I'm so sorry."

For a few weeks, he walked on eggshells around her, and she believed that he was truly remorseful, but after a Saturday afternoon at the pub, when (she later found out) he had lost a sizeable sum of money in a bet on the football, it happened again. Then again, and again, and she had lost count of the number of times, and forgotten the details. For a while, he would always say he was sorry, but he had given up saying it wouldn't happen again and, since his dad had died, he'd stopped apologising, too.

That handsome, tanned boy she had met at the dance was bigger and broader now, and his jaw was often clenched in anger, or anxiety, or fear. Elise kept their home clean and tidy, and looked after their son. How she loved looking after their son. She made herself available to her husband at the weekends, when he wanted her, and did everything she could to keep him happy. It was never enough.

All thoughts of a life outside their household had long since vanished. Maudie was always busy, anyway, and Davey had forbidden her from seeing Angela in anything other than a professional setting – as the headmistress of their son's school. Elise missed her friends dearly. But her focus was Laurie. Keeping him happy, healthy, educated, and safe. It came as a bit of a blow to discover she was pregnant again, and a small part of her wished that she might not go full-term. She just did not know how she could cope with a baby, and the long walks to and from the school, with a small boy whose legs were tired, and a tiny baby who would need to be fed, and kept clean. And how she might keep the house in order, and meals on the table. It sometimes made her head spin. Her garden was her safe space, where she could breathe, and let the combination of earth, fresh air, and the sights and sounds of the sea take over.

When Laurie was at school, and Davey out at work, she would try to find ten minutes in her day to take a cup of tea out there, whatever the weather. Sometimes, Marie would see her and come to chat. The older woman could see what was going on, but unless Elise said something to her, she was not going to tackle the subject. It just didn't do to mess in other people's business. When she saw Elise was pregnant again, she prayed for the girl, whose life was already full enough. She knew just how hard it was, bringing up children up here, in near isolation, but at least her Mick didn't hit his wife, as she knew full well Elise's husband did his, and Mick loved his kids, too. Never shouted at them like she'd heard Davey shout at little Laurie.

Although Elise was grateful for Marie's friendship, she wanted these times to herself, more than anything. To sit in the sun, or shelter in the rickety shed, and just let her thoughts drift through her mind like the clouds crossing the sea. She could remember her mum in peace, and would say sorry to her, for allowing life to turn out like this. *But you'd love Laurie, Mum*, she would think. *He is the nicest, kindest little boy you could ever meet.* And she could smile, even, to think of her son. In the peace and solitude of her garden, she would remind herself that life was not all bad.

Elise

Saturday soon comes, and I realise I've been dreading it. Working up to it. Trying to prepare myself for it.

"I'll have to get off early," Lou said on Friday evening, watching me carefully.

"I realise that, love. It's a long drive for you, all on your own."

"It is, but I don't mind driving."

"I know that," I smiled. "And we've got the summer to look forward to, if you come when Ada does. Or any other time that suits you."

"And Christmas," she reminded me.

"Oh yes, and Christmas." Without wishing to sound morbid, I don't like to take any of these things for granted, but which of us ever knows what lies ahead?

But it's so good to think I might see more of my family. My children, who are far from children, but who I once guarded fiercely, and for whom I would still lay down my life if it were required. And Ada, full of youth and enthusiasm. Like a westerly wind blowing freshly through the house.

And today, when Louisa's left, Maggie is coming, with Stevie. We're going out to the Lost Gardens of Heligan. I know she is trying to take my mind off the fact Louisa is leaving, and I am grateful for this, but I am still going to have to face returning to an empty house, sometime later today. I am used to it, of course, but my daughter's absence will be strongly felt.

As it happens, the two of them collide. Louisa is, unusually, later to leave than planned. I get the feeling that she is reluctant to go, and I'm touched.

"Come on, Lou, you need to get on your way, so you can break at Dartmoor for lunch."

"I'm coming!" she smiles down at me from the top of the stairs, bags by her feet. Again, I'm whooshed back across the years, to twenty-year-old Lou, packed up for university. It had felt like the end of the world, though I'd never have told her that.

I check my watch. It's nearly nine-thirty, which is when I'm expecting Maggie.

"My friend will be here soon, too," I say.

"Alright," Lou grins, "I won't cramp your style!"

I haven't told her a lot about Maggie. I don't know why. Actually, if I'm honest, I do. And my hunch is proved correct when there's a knock on the door and I open it to my friend – younger than Louisa herself, and similar in colouring, as Sylvia had observed. A younger version of my daughter, if you want to look at it like that. And I just know Louisa will.

"Hi, Maggie, we're just running a little bit late," I say apologetically. "This is my daughter, Louisa."

"Hi Louisa," Maggie's smile is open and guileless as always.

"Hello," Louisa says a little stiffly.

"She's about to leave for London. But we've had a lovely week, haven't we, Lou?" No matter how much I like Maggie, I want to close the door on her, draw my daughter to my chest, and just hold her. I want to tell her I love her so very much. But manners won't allow and so I stand back for her to come down into the little hallway.

"I'll just get my keys," she says to me.

"I'll wait in the car," Maggie says, considerately. "We're just round the corner. It's nice to meet you, Louisa."

"You too," Lou calls over her shoulder, slipping back into business-like mode.

I close the door onto the street. "I'm going to miss you," I say, trailing after my girl. "I've so enjoyed this week."

"Me too, Mum," Louisa turns, and I'm pleased to see she's softened down again. "Me too. And thank you, for looking after me, about AJ, you know…"

"Well, I may be biased, but the man's an idiot if he lets you slip through his fingers. Just see how things go back in London."

"Thanks, Mum. And you are most definitely biased! I think I know the score, though. Not to worry, it was fun while it lasted. And he prompted me to ask you about Dad, and I think that was a good thing."

"I think so, too." I reach for her, my girl. "I love you, Lou. I always will."

"I love you too, Mum."

"Let me know you're home safe and sound, won't you?"

"I will."

"And drive carefully."

"I always do."

I stand on the doorstep and feel my heart and stomach contract at the sight of my daughter walking off, bags in hand. I want to run after her, keep her here. I can't. I know.

Instead, I pull the door to and lock it – Louisa would be

proud – and I go to find my friend and her little girl. One day, Maggie will be watching Stevie walk away, but not just yet. They have years to enjoy.

The Lost Gardens of Heligan are as beautiful as I remember. We opt for the Pleasure Grounds, with their huge rhododendron bush boundaries and bountiful camellias. I find myself longing for a bigger garden, and time, and youth, to create something so utterly exquisite. Little ponds, paved around the outside and textured with tall green grasses and rushes quietly await discovery. Tucked into the walls are recesses where you could sit and watch the world go by, if you had the time. The summerhouse is a marvel, with views across St Austell Bay.

We wander leisurely underneath bowers, Maggie and I side by side with Stevie striding ahead, a large camera slung around her neck.

"Her new hobby," Maggie said to me.

"It's not a hobby, it's a career choice," Stevie called back.

"Little jugs have big handles," I chuckled. "Or is it 'little pitchers have big ears'? Anyway, you know what I mean."

"I do," Maggie smiled. "Not much gets past that one, I can tell you."

We watch Stevie scoot on towards one of the water features, getting up close and personal with the bubbling fountain.

"But now she definitely isn't listening, I wanted to ask if you're OK," Maggie says. "With Louisa gone and all."

"Oh yes, I'm used to it," I say. But what's the point in bluffing? "Well, I am used to it, but yes, it's hard, and I miss her. And Laurie. I haven't seen him in over a year."

"That's a long time. I can't imagine not seeing Stevie for as much as a day. But I suppose it changes when your children grow up."

"It does, because it has to. And your relationship with them changes too, of course. I do wish I could see them more easily, though. I always feel like they wanted to get away."

"Away? From you?"

"No! Well, I hope not," I laugh. "Away from the town, I suppose. There's not a lot going on, and not a lot of different opportunities. And it's quiet. Having said that, though, Laurie's living on an island with only one other human and thousands of seabirds."

"It's probably extremely noisy, then! But I know what you mean. He obviously values his own company."

"I'd say that's true. Always has been."

"How old is he?"

"Too old for you!" I flush at my own cheek, but Maggie merely grins. "I'm sorry, I don't know where that came from! He's more than ready for retirement. I have no idea what he will do when he does retire, or even if he ever will. He's always had a house with his job, so he hasn't got a place to call his own."

"Renting's OK," Maggie says.

"Oh yes, of course it is. But he hasn't got anywhere to call home. I mean, he can't live on that island forever. Well, I suppose he could…"

"That's quite exciting, then. Do you think he'll come back to Cornwall?"

"I don't suppose so, but I have let myself imagine that from time to time. I love the thought of it. But I don't want to be disappointed. And he hasn't lived here for a long, long time."

"So neither of your children ever married?" Maggie asks.

"No, neither wanted to, as far as I can make out. Louisa's had a relationship recently, which seemed promising, but it looks like that might have come to an end."

"Oh, that's a shame."

"It is, I think she really liked this one. But she's used to the single life. Like me. Maybe she'll return to Cornwall, and live in my house when I'm gone. I can't see it, somehow!"

"She could go to Caring the Community!" Maggie grins.

"Can you imagine?"

Stevie rushes to us, showing us frame after frame on the little screen of her camera.

"Those are lovely," I say, "but isn't that thing a bit heavy to have slung round your neck all day?"

"Oh no, it's fine. I'm used to it."

"I know this is really going to show my age, if my wrinkles aren't already doing that for me, but I just can't get over the way you can take so many pictures these days, and see them straightaway. When I was a girl, it was a rare treat, an occasion, to have your photograph taken. Then, when my children were your age, we used to have to put reels of film into a camera, and we only had one chance at a shot – and couldn't tell how it had come out, until the photos were developed."

"Yes, in a dark room," Stevie says airily. "I know about that process. I've been doing a course online."

I meet Maggie's eye and she shrugs. "Stevie's very

serious about this."

"I can tell. Well, good for you, Stevie. No reason you can't be a famous photographer."

"I don't think I want to be famous," she says. "That seems like a lot of hard work. But I do want to be a photographer. Or a wildlife camera person. Or both."

"Good for you," I say again. "You hold onto that dream, and see where it takes you."

As she darts off once more, this time for some close-up shots of bees milling around an abundant climbing plant, I look at Maggie.

"You seem happy," I say.

"I am. It's a beautiful day. We're in a beautiful place. And summer's on its way."

It strikes me that it's more than that, though. "Stevie seems happy, too."

"Yes, she's had a really good week at school, and I think she's bedding in more now, with all of her classmates, not just the boys. I think she just found them a bit more straightforward at first but now she's a familiar face, and I think they are starting to forget that she was ever new."

"That's good news. It must have been difficult, coming to a school partway through."

"Yes, and I've felt pretty guilty about that." A cloud passes over Maggie's face.

"Well, you mustn't," I say strongly. "Absolutely not. Children are very adaptable and she's got a good strong mum behind her. A firm foundation."

"Oh, Elise, how do you always say the right thing? I hope you're right but I don't know what's going to happen when I find a new job. I won't be here to walk her to and from school every day."

I'll miss that, I think. Though she still has no idea what a feature the two of them have been in my day-to-day life this last year or so. "She'll cope. They do the clubs before and after school, don't they? So you know she'll be looked after. And it doesn't hurt kids to see their parents working – especially their mums, I always think. Important to see women's lives don't revolve entirely around the home."

"I know. I agree, really. It's just a daunting thought. I suppose I've got used to life with my days fitting around hers, not the other way round. But I've had a couple of interviews lately and I think at least one of them went well. And... I do have some more news, actually. I... oh, this sounds so silly. I feel like a teenager. But I've kind of met somebody new."

"Really? Somebody local?"

"No. Nobody you'd know!" she laughs. "He's from out of town, but has to come here for work sometimes. And we've only really had one date, but we talk a lot – most nights, after Stevie's asleep, for hours." She can't keep the beaming smile from her face.

"Well, that sounds nice."

"It is, nice. It feels good. But it's early days, of course. And it's not like I can go and visit him, so I don't really know if it will take off."

"Why can't you visit him?" An image of a prison inmate springs to mind, but I banish it swiftly.

"Well... Stevie..." she says. "So it will probably come to nothing. It's just not practical to have a relationship, especially with someone from out of town."

"I suppose not. But if you ever need a babysitter – perhaps I should say childminder, given Stevie's age – I'd be glad to help out."

"Thank you," she says doubtfully, and I see her reluctance to trust written across her face.

"I completely understand that you might not want to do that. But the offer's there."

"Thank you, Elise," she smiles again. "I'll see how it goes."

She definitely has a spring in her step, though, and it knocks on to me, so that I find my gloom at Louisa's departure lifting. We sit out on the grass to eat our picnic. The two of them have to help haul me to my feet, as my legs have stiffened up, but it's worth it. We look around the produce gardens after lunch, marvelling at the sheer size and variety of the plants. I'm impressed at Stevie's staying power, and lack of complaining of boredom.

"That's why we brought the camera," Maggie says. "She's keen to show off to her teacher, and I knew it would keep her busy. It's been a long day, though. My feet are aching."

"Mine, too," I realise, though I hadn't given it a thought until now.

We get back into Maggie's car, and travel home in silence for the most part, broken only by the beep of Stevie's camera as she reviews her shots and deletes the ones she doesn't like.

Back at my house, Maggie has to help me again, to get out of the car. How I hate it, my body letting me down, but I'm grateful I can still do as much as I can.

"Thank you, Maggie. It's been lovely."

"I've enjoyed it, too," she says. "Will I see you on Wednesday?"

"I should think so."

"I hope you're OK, and don't miss Louisa too much. Just give me a call if you need a chat."

"Sounds like your phone line's likely to be engaged," I smile. "In the evenings, anyway."

"Ha! Yes, maybe." She glances through the window at Stevie, who luckily is absorbed in her photos. I kick myself for being indiscreet.

"Sorry. I shouldn't have said that."

"It's fine! And it's nice to have told somebody."

"Well, I'm glad that somebody was me. Thank you, Maggie. I hope you know you can trust me."

"I do. I definitely do." She goes back round to the driver's side and climbs in, then winds down the window. "Bye, Elise."

"Bye, Maggie. Bye, Stevie." The girl looks up and grins, offering an absentminded farewell.

Maggie pulls out onto the quiet road, and they are gone. I unlock the door, tired and glad now of the chance to rest, but nevertheless very aware that I am entering an empty house.

1959

Louisa had been a very different baby to her brother. He had been easy and compliant, as much as any baby could be, but Louisa was full of indignant rage, and refused to be put down, unless Elise could put her in the pram in the garden, which seemed to soothe her. However, it seemed she could still be woken by the slightest movement, and could sense if Elise was out of her approved range. She would let out an angry howl and Elise would have to pick her up, rocking and jiggling her, which Louisa reluctantly accepted was the best she was going to get.

Laurie watched his little sister carefully, and tried to placate her. And he walked obediently alongside the pram as the little threesome made their way into town on school mornings, and back again in the afternoons.

"Let him walk on his own," Davey had said, when Elise had made a comment about being tired from all the walking. It was quite a climb, to get back to the hamlet from the town. She had to do it twice a day. But at least it was keeping her fit.

Away from the road, the path became rockier and unstable, and very difficult to navigate with a pram. It took Elise close to the edge of the cliff, where there was a break in the line of trees and a view across the bay, past the town to the cliffs on the other side. Elise could see Tregynon Manor up there, sitting grey and grand, lording it over town and sea. She would sometimes stop to look, wistfully, thinking of her school days, when she had no idea just how lucky she really was. What she wouldn't give, to go back – even to the time after Annabel had died. But then, of course, she would not have Laurie and Louisa, and that would be unbearable.

Nevertheless, she could peer down between the trees that were bowed by the wind fresh off the sea, and she often imagined falling – herself and the pram, and Laurie, if he was with them. Or she imagined him watching, crestfallen, as she and his baby sister fell. She could imagine that feeling of falling, and falling, and something about it – the freedom, perhaps – almost appealed to her. But she would shake those kind of thoughts from her head.

One day, just as Elise was reaching the turn-off towards the bumpy track and her terrace – a cup of tea for her and a cup of milk for Louisa in her mind – she heard the sound of a car climbing the hill behind her.

"Elise! Elise!" She stopped, and turned. It was Maudie, and Fred.

"It's Angela," Maudie shouted from the car window. "She's been taken ill at school. She wants to see you. Climb in."

Elise didn't hesitate. She pulled Louisa from her pram, stowing it in the bushes at the side of the path, then climbed into the seat next to Fred. Maudie had moved into the back, and Elise passed Louisa to her. Maudie smiled at the little girl, who reached her hand up to touch her cheek.

Fred managed to turn the car around and had them back at school in a tenth of the time it took Elise and Laurie to walk there. An ambulance was on the school playground. It made Elise think of the ATS women, who she'd admired so much during the war. She leapt from the car, to see a stretcher being carried by two solemn ambulancemen. On the stretcher was a blanket, covering the whole of a person, including their face.

"No!" Elise breathed. Then. "No! Angela!"

Fred was there next to her, his arm around her, and Elise felt herself dissolve into spasms of grief. For Angela, for Annabel, for the dad she had never known. For the life she had once imagined, and the life she was actually living. For all of the people who had died in the war, and for Maudie and Fred, who couldn't have children of their own.

The windows of the school were lined with small, scared faces, of the children who had seen their beloved headteacher collapse in front of them, and who were now witnessing the breakdown of the mother of one of their classmates. If Elise could have seen Laurie, she would have known that he was being held back by Miss Abel, but he wriggled free of her grip and fled through the door, into the playground and towards his mother. Maudie, with Louisa in one arm, intercepted the little boy, in his shorts and school jumper. "Just hold on a second there, darling. Your mummy's just a bit upset, but she'll be alright. She'll be alright." Maudie rocked Louisa, and put her arm around Laurie, just reaching under his neck and across his chest. He watched his mum cry in Fred's arms, until she saw him, and did a double-take. She looked at her children in the arms of her best friend, and she took in the row of faces staring out at her. It shook her back to her senses. Somehow, she managed a smile.

"Hello, darling," she said to Laurie, straightening up and away from Fred, and holding her hands out to her son. "Don't look so worried. I'm alright. I'm alright."

She echoed Maudie's words, and Laurie came to her. As the ambulance drove away, Miss Abel did her best to settle her charges, and Elise managed to coax Laurie back into school. "You're better with your friends, my love. And I'll be back to pick you up, just like always. I promise."

Laurie looked dubious, but did as he was told. Maudie and Fred took Elise and Louisa back to their house, where Maudie took care of them while Fred went to work.

Elise loved Maudie's house. It had all the modern conveniences. An electric kettle, oven, and even a TV. She marvelled at it all, and how much easier this life seemed. Of course, she knew that they could afford these things in part because they didn't have children. Maudie earned a living, and they had only themselves to spend on. But Elise had no doubt that they would give it all up in exchange for a family.

She sat on the settee, drinking the brandy Maudie handed to her, and accepting cups of tea throughout the day, watching her friend play with her daughter. She felt numb, and yet somehow not surprised. It felt like life no longer had the ability to shock her.

At the end of the school day, Maudie and Elise walked together to the school, where Laurie was comforted by their enthusiastic greetings and smiles. Even his sister had a smile for him.

Maudie insisted on giving the children and Elise some tea. "Go on, Elise, it's no bother for me, and then Fred can drive you home."

"Well, alright, we'll stay for tea, thank you, but maybe we'll walk back. I don't want to be too late, and I could do with the fresh air, anyway."

In the end, Maudie walked back with the three of them, there being no sign of Fred.

"Oh, he's often late back," Maudie said. "But I know he actually is working late, not like some men."

She bit her tongue, knowing full well that Davey was often home very late – usually it was the pub that delayed him, but there had been rumours around the town, about him and other women. They were just that, though; rumours. And what good would it be to tell Elise, anyway? She wasn't about to leave him. Where would she go?

While Maudie put a shepherd's pie in the oven, Elise sat on one of the kitchen chairs and began to put her memories into words.

"I remember Angela interviewing me for Whiteleys – she was Miss Forbes then, of course."

"And your mum was there?"

"Yes, Mum was there," Elise said wistfully, her mind casting back across the years. "She and Angela already knew each other, but I never did find out how. Something to do with a mutual friend, I think. It was Angela who had told Mum about the scholarship. And she lent us some books, so Mum could help me study for the exam."

"She was a good friend. To you and your mum too, by the sound of it."

"She was," Elise looked down at Louisa, who had fallen asleep on her lap. She couldn't tell Maudie what she suspected about Annabel and Angela – could she? It wasn't the kind of thing people talked about. And would Maudie be disgusted? Was she, herself, disgusted?

It was more common than people thought, though. Elise had learned that at Whiteley; there were tales of girls kissing each other in the dormitories. But Elise had never seen anything herself, and wondered if these stories were just the product of idle, hormone-fuelled minds.

Laurie had sat in front of the television, his eyes round as saucers. When it was time to walk home, he cried.

"My legs are tired. Can't we stay with Auntie Maudie?"

"No, we have to get home, darling."

"I don't want to go home."

Nor me, thought Elise. "Of course you do, silly," she said.

"I don't. I don't like it there."

"You're just upset," Maudie said, taking Louisa from her friend so that she could comfort her son. "It's been a really strange day today, Laurie. But you get home and into your warm bed and dream some happy dreams, alright? And we'll see about you sleeping over one weekend, shall we?"

"OK," he said quietly.

"There's a good boy," Elise held him to her and pressed her face against the top of his head, remembering how it had smelled when he was a baby. He still was a baby, really, she thought.

The four of them had walked up the hill out of town, Laurie trudging tiredly, holding on to Elise's hand, Louisa fast asleep on Maudie's shoulder.

"She's heavy," Elise said apologetically. "I should carry her."

"No, you're fine. You just look after Laurie." Maudie liked the weight of the little girl, anyway. The warm solidity of her against her chest.

They didn't speak much more; too tired, and lost in

their own thoughts. Just the occasional cheery encouragement from Elise to her son, to try and chivvy him along. At the turn off to the hamlet, she insisted on taking her children from there.

"Go on, Maudie, you've still to walk back home, and won't Fred be waiting for you? He'll need his tea."

"Fred's alright, there's some shepherd's pie left in the oven. He'll find it."

"Go on, anyway. Just let me get Lou's pram."

Elise retrieved it from the undergrowth and Maudie carefully laid Louisa inside. The little girl barely stirred.

As she hugged Maudie, tears formed in Elise's eyes. She was exhausted. She just hoped that Davey would be out when she got home. She walked away and Maudie watched her go, her heart pulling towards her friend, whose hunched shoulders and downcast eyes told her everything she needed to know. Little Laurie's body language mirrored his mum's. This could not be allowed to continue.

Elise

The houses at the Saltings are nearly done. Vacant and glassy-eyed, they gaze out over the waters of the harbour. They are attracting a lot of attention and town already seems busier, although the rest of the development – the commercial stuff, as Lou calls it – will not be ready till next winter. I've noticed the roads are noisier, and the cars which pass my window are bigger, shinier. A sign of things to come.

It had to happen, I suppose. Could we really have escaped the tourist effect? Cornwall is one of the most sought-after places to live, in the whole of the UK. I get it, of course I do, but it's a luxury many can't afford, including many who are born here. As the 'For Sale' signs go up and Canyon Holdings site a shining green portacabin on the harbourside, replete with coffee machine, and curtains, soft furnishings; all brand new and beautiful according to Sylvia, whose daughter has been cleaning for them (this isn't just any portacabin, this is a Canyon Holdings portacabin), hackles are up at Caring the Community,

"Have you seen the prices those places are going for? It's criminal."

"I heard they're going for hundreds of thousands more than the asking price. People outbidding each other."

"I hope they enjoy the view, while they drown in their…

their blood money!" This last from Eleanor August, whose house, to be fair, is a short way from the new houses, which do somewhat overshadow the streets behind.

"Steady on, Eleanor!" I'd said, to be met by a look so sharp it could have cut through the new iron dock cleats on the harbour, which are not intended for use but add an air of authenticity to the place. I won't be surprised to see the new home-owners strutting about town in stripy 'nautical' tops and deck shoes. Meanwhile, the fishing fleet have been pushed further along the harbourside, almost out of sight and certainly out of hearing, so that their sometimes fruity language can't offend the sensitive ears of the incomers. But maybe they'll be cajoled into forming a sea shanty group to keep our new neighbours entertained.

Forgive me if I sound a bit cynical, but I am. Now Lou's links with AJ are cut, I feel a bit more negative about it all again. It's only half-hearted, though. Time moves on and things change. It's the way of the world. In ten, twenty years' time, all us oldies will be gone, and this new development will be embedded in the town and its culture, as though it was always here.

In the meantime, though, Maggie has got her new job, and I'm delighted for her. I'm not yet sure of the details but she says it's some kind of social enterprise work, and not too far from home. "It's just admin," she says, but I tut and tell her not to put herself down. "There is no 'just' anything." She smiles, but I mean it. I'm fed up of people belittling themselves. There are plenty of people around who'll do it for you if you let them.

It was her last day volunteering at Caring the Community, which is a shame – for us, at least. But she is happy, and things seem to be progressing with this new man of hers, as well.

I went out with her and Stevie last week, to visit the Minack Theatre, although we didn't stay all that long. An incredibly strong wind was blowing, and Maggie had a date. In fact, she had asked me to babysit Stevie.

"I'm not a baby," Stevie had protested.

"No, you're most certainly not," I said.

"I know that, Stevie," her mum consoled. "It's just an expression, isn't it?"

She had asked me on the quiet, to make sure I was happy with the idea. "I can drop you home afterwards," she'd suggested.

I had thought for a moment. "I tell you what, why doesn't Stevie come and stay with me? If she'd be happy to."

"Oh no…"

"It would be no bother. And it would mean you can have a drink, if you want to. And you won't have to worry about getting back to release the babysitter. Honestly, if you and Stevie are happy with the idea, I'd be glad to. It would be nice to liven the house up a bit."

"Really?"

"Really. But see what Stevie thinks. And I won't be offended if she'd rather stay at home."

"Oh thank you, Elise."

"It's my pleasure." And it really is. Over these last few months, I feel like Maggie has grown in confidence and stature, and her worry-worn face looks more relaxed. Fuller, somehow, in a really nice, healthy way.

To my delight, Stevie was actually more than happy to come for a sleepover, and according to Maggie was up early, packing her bag, raring to go. But first, the Minack, where Stevie and her camera battled against the wind and I tried to find a suitably sturdy and sheltered place to sit, where I wouldn't be blown away. For, while Maggie may be stronger than ever, the same cannot be said for me. I am shrinking, thanks to old age. I can feel it, and if I was to weigh myself, I know I would see it. But I've never been one for checking my weight. My skin, though, seems to become more translucent every day. My bony old hands and their rice-paper skin. But I'm OK. I'm well, and I'm happier than I have been in a long time. I would never have said I was unhappy before, but I likely wouldn't have said I was happy, either.

After the Minack, we went to a McDonald's drive-thru. I have had McDonald's before, of course, but not often. I did enjoy the novelty of it, and eating in the car. We all had something called the Veggie Deluxe, which was surprisingly tasty, though I couldn't say the same for the chips. Those aren't chips in my book – but Stevie seemed to enjoy them. Maggie had opted for the salad instead, which came in a cup, of all things. I raised my eyebrow at her. I hope she's not weight-watching for this new man of hers.

"I'm saving room for later," she said. "We're eating out round the bay, at that new place."

"The posh one?"

"Yes!" She beamed at me. "I'm a bit nervous, actually. It's not the kind of place I normally go to." She looked ruefully down at her crumb-scattered vest top.

"Don't waste your time worrying about things like that.

Just make sure you order something expensive!" I had grinned and she'd laughed.

Maggie dropped Stevie and me back at my place then she went home, to get ready for her date. I couldn't help but envy her, just a little bit, but I've had my time. The larger part of me by far was just pleased for my friend.

"Mummy's happy," Stevie observed, as we went into my house.

"She certainly seems it. And are you, my girl?"

"Yes, I'm fine," Stevie answered. "Can I go and put my stuff in my room?"

"Of course!" I followed her up, a long way behind her youthful steps. She was staying in Louisa's old room, which is seeing more life than it has in a long time. And it will soon have my Lou back in it, as well. She's coming to stay next week. Just for the weekend, but still.

Stevie unpacked her things, and set up a laptop computer so she could see the photos she'd taken that day. She showed me how it all worked, and I nodded and pretended I knew what she was talking about. She's a good little photographer, that girl. I hope she sticks with it.

In the evening, I did us both sandwiches and crisps, as we'd already had a hot meal of sorts. We watched some singing show that she likes, and then she went to bed. She was good as gold. I wasn't long after her, up to bed, but I lay awake in the dark for some time, feeling the breath of the summer whispering through the window.

1959

Back at the house, Elise was dismayed to find that Davey was home. And, of course, he had been drinking.

"Where have you been, woman?" he snarled from the armchair. *His armchair*, as he liked to think of it. It was all Elise could do to keep the disgust from her face sometimes; his good looks had been washed away by drinking and ill temper. Elise could barely believe that this man was the same person as that once seemingly easy boy, whose golden tan and charming smile had caught her attention.

"I..."

"Don't bother. I heard all about it."

"Go upstairs, darling," Elise said to Laurie, with a gentle pat on his back. She had Louisa in her arms, having stowed the pram in the little shelter outside. "I'll be right along."

"Heard all about the fuss you made," Davey said, ignoring his children entirely. "Threw yourself at your friend's husband, too, so they say. What did *Maudie* have to say about that?" he sneered.

Elise turned to go upstairs.

"Don't you ignore me!" Davey shouted, flecks of spittle spraying from his mouth as he pushed himself up from the chair. He nearly knocked over the thick brown bottle of beer that was next to his feet, and he stopped to steady it. Elise went up the stairs.

"Shhh, shhh," she comforted Laurie, who was complaining that he had not brushed his teeth, nor gone to the toilet. "It won't hurt to leave your teeth this one night, and you can use the bed pan if you need to. You get into your pyjamas, and I'll put your sister down, then come back to you."

Sleeping Louisa went easily into her cot. Elise pulled the cover over her, kissed her sweet little face, and left the room, going through to Laurie.

His worried face peered out from just above the covers, and it felt like her heart was stretching, pulling taut inside her chest.

"It's been a difficult day," Elise said, sitting on the edge of the bed. He reached his hand up to her, and she took it in hers, stroking its softness with her thumb. "A sad day."

"Yes," he said.

"But try and get some sleep now, alright? Sometimes things look better in the morning."

How this could look better, she had no idea. Life without Angela stretched ahead of her and seemed so much emptier, somehow. Then there was the immediate problem, of her husband downstairs. If she stayed long enough up here – and she always had to wait with Laurie until he fell asleep – with a bit of luck, Davey would be asleep as well.

She stayed sitting, watching her little boy's face. She felt like she could look at her children forever, and especially at moments like this, between wake and sleep. The innocence. It was gut-wrenching, and impossible to understand how it could co-exist with the nastiness in the world.

Elise used to believe in some kind of justice – good ultimately overcoming evil, but that seemed childish now, and unlikely. Yes, there was good in the world, but there was so much malice, too. The things she had heard about from the war: camps of starving people.... gas chambers... prisoners of war treated so cruelly. And closer to home – her own husband; his own father – such nastiness, on a smaller scale, perhaps, but nevertheless, where was the humanity? And how was it possible that the people who did these things had once been children, been innocent, themselves? It was a mystery greater than the never-ending nature of the universe, and space, which had once been the things that kept her awake, when she'd had nothing else to worry about.

She realised she was holding Laurie's hand a little too tightly and she loosened her grip, smiling reassuringly at him. In time, his eyelids began to flutter, until he could no longer keep them open. She continued watching him for a while, stroking his hair back, and seeing that familiar shape of his skull, which made her think of him as a baby, back when his hair had been soft and fine, and seemed like a halo around his head if the sun was behind him. She smiled to think of him then, and now, and she hoped for his future.

He did not have to be like his dad. Or his dad's dad before him. Men were not all like that, she told herself. Not taking advantage, like Lord Camelford-Bassett, or proprietary and thinking themselves entitled to say what they liked to women, like Mr Fawcett; and not bad-tempered and drunk, like Davey.

Elise looked to Fred often as her shining example of what men could, and should, be. She was determined that Laurie would be like him. She kissed her son's head and gently let go of his hand, then left the room, closing the door softly behind her. A peek in at Louisa reassured her that her daughter was still asleep, too. Now what?

She stood for a few moments at the top of the stairs, listening for the familiar snoring that would signal her husband was asleep and she was safe. She had long since given up feeling disappointed by her marriage; it was now something to be endured. She had almost forgotten that marriage was something that was meant to make people happy. Now, it was something to survive.

A soft knock on the front door startled her. She heard Davey start, and the creak of his chair as he stood up. She stayed back, in the shadows of the landing, and heard him muttering to himself as he went to open the door.

"What do you want?"

"Hello, Davey."

Maudie! What was she doing here?

"She's upstairs, putting the brats to bed."

"It's not Elise I've come to see. It's you."

Elise's heart was beating double-time in her chest. What was going on?

"Come with me, Davey. I want to talk to you."

"What? Why should I?"

"Because you don't want your children hearing this, or Elise, for that matter."

Elise held her breath.

Davey laughed. "Might have known you'd come crawling back."

Elise could just see him pulling on his shoes. *Maudie, Maudie, what are you doing?* It couldn't be what Davey thought... could it?

He shut the door carelessly behind him, not caring that it shook the house, and probably the neighbours', too.

Elise crept downstairs, though who was there to hear

her? She felt sick, and had no idea what to do. Her children were asleep upstairs, and she did not want to leave them. But she had to know what was going on. Surely… surely, her best friend was not here to tempt her husband away? Maudie hated Davey, she knew she did. But then… she had been with Davey before Elise, hadn't she? Elise shook her head, to rid herself of that idea. It made no sense. It couldn't be.

Back up the stairs she went, more quickly this time, checking both children and locking their doors. She tucked the two keys inside her dress on her way down the stairs. Slipping her feet into her boots, she opened the door and stepped out into the depths of the night, quickly closing the door behind her, and staying close to the darkness of the walls. She could hear the radio in Marie's house, and she felt a longing for the comfortable, cosy domesticity of her neighbour.

Trying to listen beyond the immediate sound of the radio, she could hear the sea, of course. It sounded appropriately angry tonight. And then… was that voices? She touched her chest, to make sure the keys were there, and crept tentatively forward. The ground was slippery, and it wouldn't do to fall and draw attention to herself.

There. A raised voice. Somewhere near the line of trees.

Elise moved towards it, quietly, softly.

"Don't be disgusting, Davey." Elise heard Maudie's voice clearly now.

"What's the matter? Don't tell me you don't want a real man?"

"Fred *is* a real man. More of a man than you could ever be, Davey Plummer."

Elise's mouth twitched with a slight smile. It had at

least stopped raining, but the branches and bushes were heavy with water, and she could feel it soaking through her clothes. Her eyes took a while to adjust to the darkness, but she could now make out the shape of her friend and her husband.

She tried to gauge where she was along the line of trees. It wouldn't do to be near that clearing, where she could picture herself slipping and falling. She pressed gently back against the comforting undergrowth, and tried to steady her breathing.

"We need to talk, Davey," came Maudie's voice.

"I don't need to listen to anything you've got to say," he spat.

"I think you do," Maudie's voice was strong and clear in the quiet night. "I won't stand by and watch you do this to my friend, and your children, any longer."

So her friend was here to give Davey a piece of her mind. Not to try and steal him away. Of course she wouldn't do that.

The world seemed to fall back into place, but Elise was worried for Maudie. She knew the extent of Davey's temper. She crept further towards them, quietly. She wanted to hear what her husband had to say for himself.

"Who do you think you're talking to?" he exclaimed. "It's none of your business, what I do with my wife, and my kids."

Elise moved as quietly as she could towards them.

"You have no idea how lucky you are, do you, Davey?" The words spilled derisively from Maudie's mouth.

"Lucky!" Davey scoffed. "With that frigid cow, and those two moaning brats? Come here."

"Don't you dare touch me," Maudie said, and it made

Elise's blood freeze. What was Davey doing to her friend?

"Don't pretend you don't want it."

"Get off me!"

"Here," she heard Davey say, "this is what a real man feels like. I'll give you that baby you want so badly."

"You bastard!" Maudie cried, and Elise broke cover, found herself moving towards their voices, without a second thought.

"Get off her, you bully. You bloody bully," she said, pounding her fists on her husband.

"Where the fuck did you come from?" Davey chuckled, easily holding her back. "Now you see what your friend's really like, sneaking up here to see me. Wants a bit of this," he clutched his groin.

"You disgust me," Maudie hissed, and she pushed him hard on his chest.

"Don't you push me, you little bitch," he said, and lunged towards her. Elise, without thinking, kicked him hard, between his legs, and he howled.

"Serves you right," said Maudie, getting up close to Davey, who was still doubled up.

"Bitch, bitch, bitch," he snarled, and straightened up. Elise moved to protect her friend, at the same time that Maudie went to push him again. In the confusion, Davey lost his footing.

Elise realised just how close they were to the edge of the path, and the little break in the trees. She reached for him, but Davey pushed her away, enraged. Elise could feel Maudie at her side, and they both put out their arms, to steady him, but the mud was thick and churned up, and he slipped again, pain and the alcohol muddling his mind and limbs.

He was in danger of falling, Elise realised. She tried again to take his arm, and Maudie did the same. They pulled him to his feet, still slipping and sliding, yet still trying to fight them off.

"You stupid bitches," he snarled. "Get your hands off me."

They looked at each other and, in a moment of madness, or possibly absolute clarity, they did as he said, and they let him go, Maudie adding a little push for good measure.

Davey cried out in surprise as the ground gave way behind him and he found himself falling, banging against a tree, then another, and unable to hang on to either. Finally, crashing onto the rocks below.

Up above, they heard it all, against the backdrop of the sea, moving restlessly below.

The scraping, and snapping, and breaking, of branches and bones, and then just the sea once more.

In the dark, Maudie looked at her friend, who promptly turned and vomited.

"What have we done?" Maudie exclaimed. "What have we just done?"

They stood, shocked, and listened, but there was nothing save for the relentless waves pushing in towards shore, and the trees dancing to the tune of the wind.

Elise, suddenly clear-headed; more than she had been in years, said, "What? We haven't done anything." She shrugged, and stepped away. "Come on, Maudie. You'd better get back to Fred. You can tell him you've been helping me look for Davey. I don't know where he is, though. Maybe he's out with one of his women."

Where was this coming from? How was Elise so calm? Was she having some kind of breakdown?

"I'll get back to the children, and I'll let you know tomorrow if Davey comes back," she continued.

"If he…?"

"Yes, yes, you know," Elise said impatiently. "He's gone missing, hasn't he? If he's not back by morning, we might have to inform the police. In case he's got hurt or something."

"Yes, right," Maudie said, pretty sure she was catching on, and that Elise had not lost her marbles but was instead starting to spin the tale that they would rely on over the next days, weeks, months and years, until they almost believed it themselves.

She couldn't stop herself shivering, though, and the rain was starting again. Maudie rubbed her foot around the muddy mire. "You're right, I'd better get home to Fred. Will you be alright?"

"I'll be fine," Elise said, although she too was shaking all over. She hugged Maudie, tightly. "And you will, too. You're the best friend I've ever had. You're like a sister to me."

"Likewise," Maudie said, hugging right back. She didn't really want to let go, because in this moment, everything felt alright, but she wondered if in the cold light of day they would regret what they had done. Could they even turn on each other? Davey was Elise's children's father, after all.

Elise was thinking of her husband, down there on the rocks. He had to have died. He must have. They would surely have heard him, otherwise. But what if he hadn't? What if he somehow clawed his way back up, and took his revenge? As long as the children were safe, that was all that mattered.

"Maudie," she said. "If anything happens to me, will you take care of Louisa and Laurie?"

"Of course I *would*," Maudie said, recovering herself in the face of her friend's fears. "But nothing will happen to you. Not now. Not now he's gone."

Tears streaming down their cheeks now, they hugged once more, then turned from each other and went their separate ways, each lost in their own thoughts and wondering if it was possible this night had really happened.

Elise

On Sunday morning, Maggie picked Stevie up, and I could tell the date must have gone well. I didn't want to ask too much, but I asked her in for a cup of tea, and she gladly accepted, seemingly keen to spill the beans to somebody.

"Shall we have it in the garden?" she asked. "Stevie, do you want to watch some telly for a while? If that's OK, Elise?" Her expression turned serious, concerned she had overstepped the mark.

"Of course, of course. That's absolutely fine. Help yourself to biscuits, Stevie. That is, if it's OK with you, Maggie?"

She laughed. "We're far too polite with one another, aren't we? I am more than happy for you to offer my daughter biscuits, any time you like."

"And you are very welcome to switch the TV on for her, and just make yourselves at home. I like having you around."

"We like it too, don't we Stevie? In fact, if it wasn't for you, I don't think I'd feel anywhere near at home as I do now."

I felt a warm glow at these words. I poured boiling water onto our teabags, swishing them about, then fishing them out with a spoon. A splash of milk, and we were ready to go.

"Did you have a good night?" I asked, once we were out in the garden. It was a blue-skied day, the sun regal and blessing us all with its rays.

"I did, thank you," she could barely keep the smile from her face. "We just get on so well."

"And is he handsome?"

"Yes! Well, I think so. He's a bit older than me, but I quite like that, you know. And he's talking about moving here. Well, he kind of has to, with his job."

"Now, that sounds exciting."

"I think it is. I mean, I don't want to rush into anything. And I wouldn't, with Stevie..."

"I know. I know she's your priority, but it's OK to have something for yourself, you know. Someone."

"It is, isn't it? And Tony's so great. Oh god, I sound like a teenager. I feel like a teenager."

She looked like one, for a moment. Her cheeks flushed and a light in her eyes. Clearly Tony is a bit of a hit.

"But Elise, what do you think? Really? I had made up my mind not to even think about relationships until Stevie's a bit older."

"Maggie, you can't always plan these things. Life takes its own course. You don't know who you're going to meet, or when. If you like him, and he's good to you, then see where it goes. Just remember, you have a choice. And you deserve to be happy."

"I don't know if that's true." Her eyes are downcast for a moment, and I feel my heart go out to her. What is it with these young women? Maggie, and my Louisa? Why don't they realise their full worth? That any man would be lucky to be with them. And that they only deserve a man who knows this.

"Maggie, you're a good person. A great friend to me. Honestly, you and Stevie have lifted me so much. I suppose I'd... not given up, exactly, but given in. Accepted a somewhat empty life. You helped me start filling it again. I hope you know how grateful I am."

It's true. I love my family – Laurie, Louisa and Ada – in a way that could never be replicated, or surpassed. I would drop anything, for any of them, and I feel more sure than ever that they will carry some of my spirit on in life, and some of my mum's, too.

I cannot wait to see Louisa next weekend, and Ada in a few weeks' time. And if we can pull off Christmas together with Laurie as well, I think I could say I will die a happy woman, and not be exaggerating. But I can't spend all my time just waiting for their visits. I have no idea how much life I might have left, and I want to get the most I can from every single drop of it.

I realise that I may see less of Maggie, once she's started this new job, and once Tony is in town. And in September, Stevie starts at the secondary, half an hour away. I won't see them passing by my window anymore. But Maggie assures me we will still have our days out, and Stevie says she's going to pop in to see me sometimes when she's hopped off the bus from school.

I will look forward to that.

The aftermath

If the two young women had been close before, in the wake of Davey's death (**Tragic accident of local businessman**, ran the headline in the *Advertiser*), their friendship only grew closer.

They stuck to the line about Davey being missing, but as Elise said, this had not seemed unusual at first. The town gossips for once came in useful and were able to verify that Davey very often was out in the pub, or off with some floozy ("Only, no need to tell Mrs Plummer about this, eh? She's got enough on her plate.")

It was only in the morning that Elise awoke to find he had not returned at all, and Marie, Elise's neighbour, had seen the muddy mess at the top of the cliff, and the nearby vomit, which suggested Davey had not been well. She bore witness to this at the inquest, after Davey's body had been recovered by the lifeboat, having been washed out to sea by a rising tide. There was no sign of foul play; just an unfortunate accident, which some said was waiting to happen, given the amount that man drank.

A verdict was given of death by misadventure, and the town gathered closer around Davey's widow, making her feel a part of it in a way she never had before.

The two funerals – Angela's and Davey's – were held just a week apart, and Elise felt profound and genuine grief at both.

She did not miss Davey one bit, but having to stand alongside his mother, who cried real, raw tears, was terrible. This was what Elise had dreaded. She felt desperately sorry for the other Mrs Plummer, who had endured a marriage of violence and abuse. Her tears provoked Elise's, who felt sincere sorrow for the young man she'd met all those years ago, and how his life had turned out.

She fervently believed it was the upbringing he'd had, with his own violent father, which was to blame for how he had turned out, but that could never be an excuse. Davey had his own mind, and his own free will. Elise was glad that now her children would not suffer the same fate. Instead, she was determined to give them a steady, loving home. She would not spoil them, but she would try to understand them, and she would set them a good example.

This began with finding a job. It would be good for both her children, son and daughter, to see their mother working. She wanted to be a role model for Louisa, who should never feel confined to marriage, motherhood and home-making. And she wanted Laurie to see that women were just as capable as men. Her greatest fear was that, as Davey's son, he might turn out like his dad, but she really need not have worried.

Mr Fawcett was good enough to take Elise back on, although as he kept telling her, "This is not charity. You're one of the best workers I've had. And you know the business inside out. Enough of these flighty young girls."

Elise, still in her twenties, was hardly what you'd call old, but she laughed.

"You're not like them, Elise. You never were. I'm glad you're back."

Her status as a widow seemed to offer her even more protection than being married to a living person had. Mr

Fawcett was kind and courteous. Elise took on the management of the younger girls and, should his manner towards them ever become less than professional, a cough and a stern look pulled him back into line. In time, his son Nigel joined the firm, and he was a breath of fresh air. More worldly-wise, having been to Edinburgh for his studies, and spent a year backpacking afterwards; something which was much more unusual in those days than now. He wanted to use his legal work for the good of society, and introduced the concept of legal aid to the firm. Mr Fawcett had half-hoped Nigel and Elise might find some common ground, but Elise had a feeling that she wasn't Nigel's type.

Mr Fawcett allowed Elise to work school hours only, and Maudie looked after Louisa while Elise was at work. She could fit her own work in around the girl, she said, and anyway, it was a pleasure to have her company. Elise was more than pleased that her daughter had another strong female role model in her life, and she believed that not being with her mum all day would make Louisa more outward-looking.

As for the cottage on the cliff, this stood empty once more. Angela had left her house to Elise, who wasted no time moving into the neat little terraced house on Godolphin Terrace, feeling the safety in numbers of the town. Close to the harbour, and the shops, and her friends. Just a short walk to the school, compared to what she had been used to.

Elise thanked her lucky stars for bringing Angela into her life, although really she had only to thank her mum. Somehow, Annabel had found a way to look after her daughter, although she had been gone now such a long time.

As the years trod on, and the children grew, Elise worked longer hours. She went to night classes – an A-Level in law, and various art classes. She transformed the previously untouched attic into a little studio, and loved climbing the ladder to the top of the house, where she had a window put in, allowing her an uninterrupted view of the sea. Laurie and Louisa transformed into near-adults and both left home, with their own sure, steady paths to follow.

The house was empty, and Elise missed her children so much that she ached, but at the same time, she knew she had set them on the right path and her heart swelled at the thought. Nobody was a perfect parent, but she had done her best.

And all the while, never far from her side, was Maudie. The best friend she could ever have wanted. Fred was a dear friend, too, and they often included Elise on their holidays; abroad or further upcountry. They were happy to have her with them, and she never felt like a third wheel. They would never let her.

The decades marched onwards, and Elise's hair turned grey, and wiry. Maudie dyed hers till the end, not wanting to give in to old age, and yet, after Fred died, she grew older more quickly than Elise, it seemed; ill health plagued her, and her body gradually grew frail.

Elise was worried. Laurie, too, but particularly Louisa, who regarded Maudie as a second mum. What would they have thought, had they known what Maudie and Elise had done to their father? It never mattered, because the truth of what had happened to Davey went with Maudie to her grave.

When she died, their hearts broke in unison, and of all the tragedies to have happened to Elise, it was this that she felt the most. Life became hollow. They did not love each other as Annabel and Angela perhaps had; and Fred was undoubtedly the love of Maudie's life, but there is room for many types of love in the world.

After Davey, Elise never married again and had only the occasional romantic encounter, which never amounted to much. It was always her children, and her friends, who made her smile.

Coming Soon:
Maggie (Connections Book Two)

Maggie

I am starting to feel really bad that I haven't been entirely honest with Elise. It's just that, as time goes on, it's becoming increasingly difficult to tell the truth. And I know she's got this particular image of me, which I haven't done much to correct. To her, I'm just a hard-working single mum, with an unsupportive family, and Stevie is the product of a failed relationship with an unreliable, useless man.

Now, some of these things are true. I am a hard-working single mum, and Stevie's dad is completely unreliable, and useless, at least as far as I'm concerned. But then that is only a part of the truth. As with many people's stories, it's not altogether straightforward. And I worry what Elise would say if she knew the whole of it.

I like the 'me' that she sees. Especially compared to how my best friend, and my own mum and sister, feel about me at the moment. Not Mum, maybe, but certainly Julia and Stacey.

And I never meant to lie to Elise, but when we talked that time, at Lanhydrock, and I started to get an idea of what her marriage had been like, I just couldn't bear to tell her the whole truth. She has been through so much, and been so strong. And I've just been a fool. But for some reason, I let her think otherwise. I suppose I liked her sympathy.

There have been times when I've hated myself, but I know that's of no use, and I seem to have inherited Dad's ability to bounce back. A survivor's instinct. Which is important for me, and for Stevie. I may have let down most of the people I love, but I've never let her down, and I don't intend to start now.

This is why I'm taking it slowly with Tony. I do really like him, but we've been there before, haven't we? Honestly, I can physically cringe when I think of what I've been like in the past. Always so keen for boys to like me at school, when I knew deep down that they really only wanted to know me to get closer to Stacey, or Julia. It only made me try harder. Like I say – cringe.

So I'll take it slow. Until I get to know him. His past. Does he have secrets of his own? He's been married, he says, no kids. Why is this? Did they not want them? Did he want them, and not her? Or the other way round? Was he a philanderer? A work-addict? A good, old-fashioned bastard?

I feel bad thinking those things about him, but really, I don't know him do I? I suppose, if this lasts, and if he really is all that he seems to be, I will have to face telling him the truth, too. Maybe he'll pass all of my requirements – I hesitate to say 'tests' – with flying colours, and then I'll blow it all with the truth about me, and alienate him like I've alienated all the other people I care about. Except for Stevie. And now Elise. And what will happen when Elise finds out, as I suppose she must?

I just can't bear the idea of Stevie seeing me for the weak woman I am. But I'm kidding myself if I think we can go through life without her finding out. And I can't keep her away from Mum, or Julia, forever. I just hope they do still care enough about me, or Stevie at the very least, to keep their mouths shut.

I'm getting quite stressed out, thinking about it all. Putting all the personal stuff aside, very soon I am going to have to tell Elise about my job, and who I'm working for, because it's going to be obvious. But having heard all the incredibly strong – almost unanimously negative – opinions about the Saltings, around town and while I was volunteering at Caring the Community, when the truth comes out about my new role, I fear I'm not going to be very popular.

Tied up with this new development, changing the face of the town forever. I've been offered a great job, and I genuinely think I can help make everything work better for people in the town. I just know it won't be seen like that, though. I am scared I'll be seen as a traitor, just when I'm starting to feel at home here.

Acknowledgements

In my last book, *Weathering the Storm* (Book One of the Coming Back to Cornwall series) I actually omitted to thank my amazing, talented, lovely friend and cover designer, Catherine Clarke. Her beautiful covers play a fundamental part in catching people's attention, and I absolutely love the cover for *Elise*. So I am mentioning her first, before I risk forgetting again! Thank you for everything, Mrs Clarke.

Next up, we have my team of beta readers, who have kindly given up their time to read the first draft of the book, and feed back to me their responses, so I can hopefully polish the story and the text to make it shine when I release it into the wider world. Thank you, Marilynn Wrigley, Jean Crowe, Amanda Tudor, Yvonne Carpenter, Helen Smith, Clare Coburn, Ginnie Ebbrell, Tracey Shaw, Joanna Blackburn and Rebecca Leech. I hope you know how much I appreciate all your help, honesty and encouragement.

Hilary Kerr, thank you so much as always for your brilliant editing advice and correcting of errors! Thanks also for being there to bounce ideas off when it came to getting our Ash this year. A shared love of border collies and books is a great place for a friendship to start.

Pat Pearce is somebody who I have got to know through my work, though we have yet to meet in person! Pat's mum was drafted over to Cornwall with the ATS during the Second World War and Pat very generously entrusted me with a copy of an interview her mum gave relating to this time in her life. I was hugely touched by Pat's faith in me to look after the tape and the notes, which are fascinating, and give a lovely insight into the woman Pat's mum must have been, as well as the time that she lived through.

Gill Corbett and Beryl Gibson also deserve a special mention as two people I have got to know over the last year, thanks to my books, while my mum was ill, and after she died. Thanks and love to you both.

Caroline Brennan and Esther Harris at Bookollective, for your expertise, support and general brilliance in the world of PR. I hope that this is the first of many times we work together.

To my dad, Ted Rogers, special thanks for being my proofreader on all of my books, and for being nitpicky about the finer details! It's been a tough, tough year, and I'm glad we have been able to get through it together.

And finally, my family: Chris, Laura and Ed. We've been locked down, locked in, through some of the worst times of our lives, and we've survived. Not only have we survived, but we've been able to have some fun, topped off by Ash, the canine cherry on the cake.

Actually, that is not quite the final part of these acknowledgements. My final thanks go to all of you who have read my books, and if you've read this far you've shown a real commitment! To those of you who enjoy my books, you've helped to make one of my dreams come true, and that's pretty amazing, so thank you.

(I do have another dream, of one day, eventually, living in Cornwall... for now, I think I'll just have to carry on writing about it.)

Also by Katharine E. Smith:

The bestselling Coming Back to Cornwall series:

Writing the Town Read - Katharine's first novel.

"I seriously couldn't put it down and would recommend it to anyone to doesn't like chick lit, but wants a great story."

Looking Past - a story of motherhood, and growing up without a mother.

"Despite the tough topic the book is full of love, friendships and humour. Katharine Smith cleverly balances emotional storylines with strong characters and witty dialogue, making this a surprisingly happy book to read."

Amongst Friends - a back-to-front tale of friendship and family, set in Bristol.

"An interesting, well written book, set in Bristol which is lovingly described, and with excellent characterisation. Very enjoyable."